L.P. Simone

CHARLOTTE'S GHOSTS

The Mystery of the Vanishing Boy

L.P. Simone
info@lpsimone.com
www.DragonSongPublishing.com

Ordering Information:
Quantity sales. Special discounts are available on quantity purchases by libraries, schools or other services designed to promote literacy and the creative exploration of the written or spoken word. For details, contact the author at the address above.
Orders by U.S. trade bookstores and wholesalers.
Printed in the United States of America
Simone, Louise Pisano.
Charlotte's Ghosts: The mystery of the vanishing boy
188 p. cm.
ISBN 979-8-9878699-3-2
1. —Children's Stories Fiction —Historic Fiction —U.S. Civil War. 2. Paranormal Fiction. 3. Ghosts

Library of Congress Control Number
2024926795

DEDICATION

To everyone who listened while I struggled to tell this story, especially Maryrita Wieners, my first writing teacher and friend, David, Jana, and my mother and father whose love I feel still even after all this time.

The Reviews are in.

"Simone's emotional prose and vivid descriptions...bring the narrative to life,right up to the affecting conclusion." ~ *Kirkus Reviews*

"Simone artfully navigates the dual storylines of C.C. in the present and Jeremy Turner, a boy from the Civil War era, creating a rich tapestry of interconnected lives."~*Literary Titan Book Award*

"**Charlotte's Ghosts** is a great selection for teens or older readers who enjoy a historical element in a coming-of-age story."~*Reader's Favorite*

Opening Events of The Civil War
1860-1862

1860 **November 6, 1860 - Lincoln Elected 16th President**

After years of contentious politics, Abraham Lincoln won the Presidency of the United States. Branded an abolitionist by Southerners, many Southern states failed to even provide ballots with Lincoln as an option. Lincoln campaigned on the premise that slavery was immoral and against the founding principles of the Republic, and that he would prevent its expansion, but he had no firm plans on how he would be able to end it.

December 20, 1860 - South Carolina Secedes

1861 **January 9-26, 1861 - Multiple States Secede**

Mississippi, Florida, Alabama, Georgia, and Louisiana secede

February 1-9, 1861 - Confederate Formation

February 1: Texas Secedes
February 4: Seceded States Convene in Alabama
February 8: Confederate Constitution adopted
February 9: Jeff Davis elected provisional President of Confederacy

March 4, 1861 - Lincoln Inaugurated

April 12-17, 1861 - War Begins

April 12: Fort Sumter fired upon
April 13: Fort Sumter surrenders
April 17: Virginia State Government votes to secede - Governor calls out volunteers to defend Virginia

May 1861 - Further Secession and Military Action

May 6: Arkansas and Tennessee secede
May 20: North Carolina secedes
May 23: Virginia officially secedes
May 24, 2:30 AM: Federal Troops enter Virginia and take Alexandria
May 31-June 1: Skirmish at Fairfax Courthouse

June 17, 1861 - Vienna Ambush

Union soldiers of the 1st Ohio Regiment are ambushed near Vienna, VA

July 21, 1861 - First Battle of Bull Run

First Battle of Bull Run / Battle of Manassas â€" Confederate forces under Thomas "Stonewall" Jackson help drive Union troops back toward Washington

1862 **August 28-30, 1862 - Second Battle of Bull Run**

Second Battle of Bull Run / Battle of Manassas - Another Confederate victory

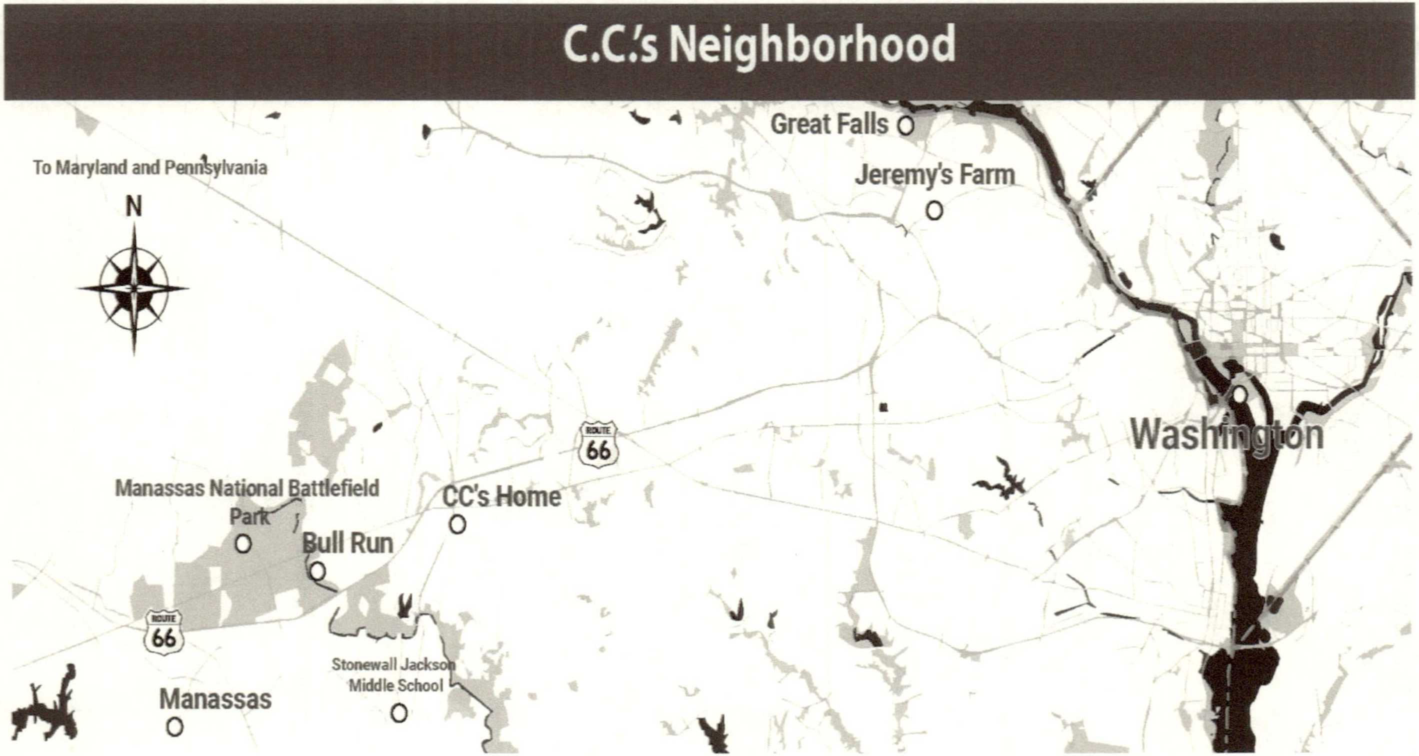

C.C.'s Neighborhood

Great Falls
To Maryland and Pennsylvania
Jeremy's Farm
N
ROUTE 66
Washington
Manassas National Battlefield Park
CC's Home
Bull Run
ROUTE 66
Stonewall Jackson Middle School
Manassas

1

CHARLOTTE

August 29, Manassas, Virginia

BEAU AND I ARE BREATHING HARD AND SWEAT STREAMS off my face. The hill in front of us blocks our path home. Well, at least, what's home now. My real home is thousands of miles away.

And it's not home anymore, anyway.

Ahead, I can make out a statue of a guy on horseback. He's the imaginary finish line. The flanks of his bronze horse dull the light of the evening sun. I swear, no matter what people say about Arizona's desert heat, summers in Northern Virginia ought to be outlawed. How anyone breathes this soup is a total mystery.

"C'mon, Beau," I say. The look he gives me, with his tongue lolling out, and his black fur gleaming in the sun, says, "You got to be kidding me" as clearly as words.

"You're right," I say to him, "I don't know why I bother."

In one of his last emails, Dad sent a training schedule that he was supposed to be home for. It was to get me ready to try out for the Cross-Country team. I guess he'll never know if I make the team or not, which means he won't know I didn't train hard enough, either.

And that means I'm not letting him down.

I swallow hard and start up the hill, slowly.

The trip up the hill isn't a sprint, but it's the best I can do.

Although Cross-Country wasn't football, like he played, according to him, it was the best option for a girl.

And now everything has changed. I live in Northern Virginia, and Dad will never be coming home.

The sign by the base of the statue says the guy on the horse is Thomas "Stonewall" Jackson. He and his Virginia brigade threw back Lincoln's troops and stopped the Union advance into Virginia in the first battle of the Civil War, "like stones in a wall."

So, this must be the guy my new school is named after.

It's hard to believe my parents grew up here. But the whole Confederate general thing explains a lot. The way he looks, sitting there on his horse like a god, you'd think the South won or something.

A cloud of gnats buzzes around my head, and my heart's rhythm matches the tempo of Beau's panting. I wipe my face with the hem of my shirt. Beau tugs me across the parking lot to the water fountain mounted on the wall of the Visitor's Center. With a twist of the handle the water leaps over the basin. Beau's head goes sideways to lap at the stream as it splashes on the cement. It's so sweet, I laugh, then catch myself.

Lately, laughter feels like treason.

I look out over the hill we just climbed. Mom's unpacking.

She says the sooner we get things put away the sooner things will feel like home. She's said the same thing every time the Army moved us. This time is completely different, thought. This time, all Dad's stuff went on a Goodwill truck back in Arizona.

No matter how many times she says it, Manassas will never be home.

My shadow stretches clear across the parking lot making me cringe. Five-feet-seven is too tall for 7th grade, and now, even the sun's making me feel like a freak.

Dad was tall.

I lean in over the arc of water and pull on my ankle to stretch my quad. Water mingles with the salt on my lips before it slides past an ache in my throat that never seems to go away.

After a couple of gulps of water, I take a deep breath. "Be brave, soldier."

It's what Dad said before every deployment. Even with all the videos we have of him, sometimes I can't remember what his voice sounded like.

Beau watches as the barn swallows twitter and swoop low in front of a horizon streaked with rose and gold, and his tail sways high behind him. The scent of dried grass hangs thick in the air. How creepy is it that there's a park where all those people fought?

And died.

I'd bet you a billion dollars no one will ever build a park like this in Afghanistan. Not in a million years.

I slurp another mouthful of water and let the water splash over the side again for Beau. My hamstrings twitch.

"You gotta run every day, C.C." It was practically all Dad talked about the last few times we spoke, back when we thought he'd be home for tryouts.

A tree beyond the building sways and the leaves whisper. Hoping to catch whatever breeze might be trying to fight through the heat, I lift my arms out to my sides. Mom says storms come up pretty quickly around here. But there's not a wisp of a cloud in sight. The gust moves Beau's fur.

As we turn toward the road, I notice a kid, a little older than me, sitting on the wall that borders the Visitor's Center's outdoor patio a couple feet away. He's got his head in his hands and his elbows are resting on his legs.

Funny, he wasn't there a minute ago.

Most boys my age are a lot shorter than me. Or tall and skinny. Not this guy. Sweat plasters his shirt to him and you can see every muscle in his back. His sleeves are rolled up above his elbows, and even his wrists and forearms look strong. Blue veins stand out against pale skin.

The super strange thing, though— he's wearing a pair of thick grey wool pants. With suspenders.

I step away. Even though *he* snuck up on *me*, I'm give him plenty of space. But good old Beau has other ideas. Before I can stop him, my dog lunges toward the kid, tugging me along with him, and he knocks the kid's elbow with his nose.

"Beau!" I yank him back, but he's gotten what he wanted. The boy goes down on his knees, and hugs Beau like they're long-lost buddies.

"Sorry," I say, giving Beau some leash. "He's really friendly."

The boy doesn't seem to hear me. He's got his face buried in Beau's neck, and he's muttering something. Beau sits down quietly. His tail scrapes the ground behind him. "Blue, you crazy dog," he says. "You found me!"

"It's Beau, actually," I say as my dog slobbers all over a stranger.

I step forward to grab Beau's harness. The boy smells of the forest, like moist earth, and a scent that reminds me of the Fourth of July. Dead leaves and a twig cling to his hair. It's like he's been rolling around in the woods, and now that I'm closer, his pale skin seems almost transparent.

"So, do you go to Stonewall Jackson?" I ask, then cringe. *God, C.C. You just met this guy.*

The boy looks at me. His eyebrows knit together, and a muddled look crosses his face. A strand of matted, blond hair falls across his eyes, and splotches of something dark are smeared across his face.

"I'm not Thaddeus," he says.

And then, I swear to God…he disappears.

Jeremy

April 18, 1861, Fairfax County Courthouse, Virginia.

Sweat trickled down Jeremy's neck and spine. Spring wasn't even a month old, and already the sun felt like it would fry him. He lowered the plow's handles and hitched his shoulders to keep the reins from falling. Pa bent over the blade's front bracket and hoisted it out of the mud.

Ginny was old, but she'd make it through spring planting. Muddy red dirt splayed out on both sides of the plow's hilt emitting the rotting grass and sharp tangy smell of Virginia clay. Virginia had its very own particular smell.

Smells like home, Jeremy thought.

Pa resettled the plow's blade, and Jeremy grabbed the handles again. "Come on, girl." He made a soft clicking sound in the back of his throat. "We've only got a few more rows."

Good thing she can't count, otherwise, she'd stop right here and refuse to take another step. Ginny's flesh twitched, and her tail whistled through the air striking her back with a *thwick*. She strained against the harness.

"Good girl, Ginny."

From the corner of his eye, Jeremy saw Blue raise his head off his paws. The dog was asleep in the shade, but something had caught his attention. He stared down the lane toward the road. Jeremy followed Blue's stare. Will Dawson was hollering and waving something over his head.

Blue stood and watched as Will approached. Then he was off in a flash, like he was after a rabbit. The dog raced toward Will, his black coat luminescent-blue in the sun, mud flying from under his feet. Jeremy smiled. Blue would never walk if he could run. The dog pulled up short in front of Will and barked the high-pitched bark that meant he was happy to see you. Pa and Jeremy stopped struggling with the plow. Ginny sighed. Her tail whipped past Pa's face.

"Blue!" Jeremy called to him. "It's Will Dawson for goodness' sake, you crazy dog."

"I ran all the way here," Will gasped and handed a broadsheet to Pa. His words were punctuated by gasps. "It's done . . .They voted. . .Virginia seceded. The Governor's . . . called up . . . the militias…Meeting tonight." He squinted up at them. "Pa sent me over…to tell thee. Master Janney has called a Meeting. Tonight."

Jeremy watched Pa studying the paper. He wiped the front of his shoulder across his face. "What do we do, sir?" he asked.

Pa didn't speak for a long time. When he handed the paper back to Will he said, "I thank ye for the news, Son. I expect ye ought to go on home now. I expect there are still chores to be done with thy pa."

Jeremy started at Pa's words. Pa wasn't a Quaker like Ma.

When they married, the Fairfax Meeting expelled her on account of Pa's father and brothers all being officers in the United States Army. "Ye" and "thy" sure sounded odd coming from him.

Jeremy squinted into the distance as Will Dawson trudged back across the neatly plowed field. "Are you gonna fight, Pa?" Jeremy asked. A lilt of excitement crept from his heart to his voice. Jeremy studied Pa. "Are you gonna fight for President Lincoln?"

"I don't aim to do anything until we finish plowing this field, Son." Pa turned back toward Ginny whose ears twitched off a fly. "Didn't you tell this animal we only had a few more rows left? A field don't plow itself."

"Yes, sir." Jeremy bent and wrapped his hands around the plow handles. The wood bit into his calluses. Whatever happened now that Virginia had chosen a side would have to wait until this field was plowed.

"Get on now, Ginny," he said and leaned toward the horse's rump. "A field don't plow itself."

2

CHARLOTTE

I SPRINT HOME. NOW I DON'T EVEN NOTICE THE HEAT.

That kid had been sitting right there. Beau saw him, too.

"Crazy dog." I say looking at him running beside me "You started it." I shake my head, ignoring a sharp kick in my chest.

But what exactly did he start?

I don't slow down until I turn up the front path to our house. Mom's car is in the driveway.

I take the four steps of our porch two at a time with Beau right beside me. We leap across the deck and the screen door crashes into the frame as it swings closed behind us.

"Mom?" I call.

"I'm in here, Charlotte." She pokes her head out of the kitchen. A long red apron covers her work clothes. She's holding a hunk of raw ground meat.

"Mom, something weird just happened. On the Battlefield." How do I explain this? "We were running near that statue of the guy on the horse... There was a kid ...and he..."

"Slow down, slow down." Mom blows a stray hair out of her face. "You're talking too fast. Look at poor Beau! Give him some water for heaven's sake. He's overheated."

I fill Beau's bowl, but before I can say anything else, Mom's cell phone rings.

She takes a deep breath. With her hands extended in front of her, palms up, covered in ground beef fat, she says. "Get that, will you sweetheart?"

"It's Mrs. Tuckerman," I say, Mom's new boss. She nods, and I tuck the phone between Mom's shoulder and ear, as she wipes her hands on her apron.

"Hello, Dona," she sings into the phone. She mouths to me, "Dinner in 15 minutes." Mom looks down at Beau. "Feed the dog" she signals and turns around to listen to her boss.

I stare at Mom's back. I don't know what I expected. It's not like I can explain what happened, anyway. And I can guess what she'd say.

First, she'd tell me that I've been under a lot of stress with the move and "everything." And then she'll say, "Oh C.C., don't be so melodramatic. I'm sure there's a perfectly good explanation. People don't just disappear."

I go over the whole scene in my head. The kid was probably a re-enactor or something. She talked the whole drive from Arizona about how much I was going to love Virginia. "It's so full of history. Loads and loads of Civil War reenactments every summer." How when she was a little girl "my daddy rode around on a great big horse pretending to be a Rebel general," she laughed. "Folks down there are still fighting that old war." The closer we got to Virginia, the more her Southern accent came back.

Jeremy

Ma's voice broke into Jeremy's dream of sitting with Caroline under the oak tree while Blue chased birds by Old Man Carter's pond. Then he ran across the back pasture toward home, fighting to wake up. Caroline was gone but something heavy held him down. He struggled under its weight, and breaking free, opened his eyes. Lying hard against his back, on top of the covers, Blue snored. Jeremy couldn't move.

His parents spoke in hushed voices as they sat at the dinner table, haloed, and silhouetted by the moon's pale light coming through the window. Silver splashed across the tablecloth and the bare floor.

"John Gabriel Turner, you can't up and leave the farm like that," Ma whispered. Jeremy held his breath. "It's the start of spring planting."

"I'm not going to sit by while others fight. It's my duty to go. President Lincoln's called up troops." His father's voice grew louder as he spoke.

"Shhhhhhhh!" Mother looked over at the bed where Jeremy slept. He snapped his eyes closed. Blue snored. Good old Blue. His snoring always fooled them. They'd be hoppin' mad if they caught him listening. Jeremy ducked his face under the patchwork quilt that covered him. When they started whispering again, he risked a quick peek.

"Virginia called out the militia. They aim to fight Lincoln. If they're mustering troops too, they're going to make me join up." Pa's voice sounded cross. Jeremy couldn't remember a time when his father had raised his voice to his mother.

Pa's voice softened. "Laurie, you're not a member of any Meeting. And I never was. I might not be an officer like my brothers, but I am no Quaker, neither." His shoulders slumped. "You can't expect me to sit by and let other men die."

Ma shushed Pa again, pressing her index finger against her lips and glancing back at the bed. Pa stood. The chair scraped on the hard floor. He looked down at Ma, and she snatched his hand, clasped it in both of hers, and laid it against her cheek.

"I've got to go." Pa's voice rang with a firmness Jeremy knew well. Pa didn't chew on decisions. He acted. But there was something else in is voice. Sadness maybe. "It's my duty," he said. "I stand with Lincoln on this. It's time we end the abomination of slavery."

Ma didn't answer. She clasped his hand to her heart. Pa put his other hand on her shoulder then knelt down in front of her. He pulled her to him.

"What about Jeremy?" Ma asked as Pa backed away.

"He's just a boy. Even secessionists won't force a child to fight."

"War and killing are sins, John." Now fear rang in Ma's voice.

"So is calling another man your property." Pa glanced over at Jeremy who squeezed his eyes shut again. "I aim to be to Philadelphia before the devils even know I'm gone. I'll leave at first light."

"It's a sin." Ma sounded like she couldn't breathe.

Pa didn't answer for a long time. Then he said, "I'll send word when I can." He strode past Jeremy's bed, his long arms swinging at his side, and heavy shoes clomping hard on the floor planks. The cabin door opened. Cricket and bullfrog song swelled. Sweet night air swept over the bed and Blue's snoring stopped. The dog lifted his head. The covers pinning Jeremy released. Blue staggered, then turned around. His claws scratched at Jeremy's back and shoulder through the quilt, before the dog jumped off the bed, shifting the corncobs in the mattress. Blue landed with a clack of claws on the wooden floor.

Her skirts swishing, Ma moved across the room. The night sounds grew louder as she let Blue out to follow Pa.

A moment later, the mattress shifted again. Ma sat down at Jeremy's feet. She lowered her head to the quilt. With his eyes nailed shut, Jeremy tried not to breathe as Ma's sobs shook the bed beneath him.

3

CHARLOTTE

I THINK ABOUT THE DISAPPEARING BOY ALL NIGHT. MOM doesn't care about what got me all fired up, and I don't tell her, so I suppose we're even.

Dad would have asked.

Now I'm lacing on my running shoes for Cross-Country tryouts ...at the crack of dawn. Okay, so 8:00 am isn't the crack of dawn, but it might as well be for all the sleep I got last night. Every time I closed my eyes, all I saw was the boy's eyes. There one second and gone the next.

Just like that.

My heart thinks I'm already sprinting, it's beating so hard.

I lean on the gate to the school's track, and it whines under my weight. The air smells of freshly mowed grass.

No one at this school knows a thing about me. If we keep it that way, I won't have to listen to people say how sorry they are all the time.

Across the field, some workmen are painting the bleachers. A few kids loosen up in a knot on the 20-yard line of the football field. A thin older guy with a clipboard and a whistle motions for us to gather around him in a circle. I trot up and stand behind a girl with a blond ponytail. "My name is David Elsberry," he says. "I have the pleasure of coaching the Cross-Country team here at Stonewall Middle School. Practices are Monday, Wednesday, and Friday immediately after school. We may not be as glamorous as the football team, but we take meets very seriously. If you make the team, you'll be expected to make every practice, no excuses.

"That's why we regularly finish in the top three in the league." He glances over both shoulders as if to see who's listening. "That's more than you can say about the football team.

"Okay." He checks his clipboard. "Today, folks, I want to see how you run. Anyone can run fast when properly trained, but this is a tryout." Sweat glistens on his upper lip. "Don't kill yourselves. We'll save that for the meets..." He pauses. "Got it?"

Some kids nod. Others kick the grass. Me, I'm wondering what I'm doing here. I could turn around and walk away. Dad would never know.

End of story.

"Okay," Coach Elsberry says, and glances at his clip board again, then back at us. "Isabel Price is our girls' team captain." A strawberry blonde standing to his left straightens, smiles, and gives a small wave with a flick of her wrist.

"And Josh," Coach says, "is the boy's team captain." He checks the group. "Josh?"

"Here, Coach." I jump like I've been poked in the side. Josh is standing right behind me.

The whole group stares. I step out of the way.

Josh moves to the center of the circle. Like the Battlefield Boy, Josh Gerber is thin and anything but gawky. His shirt hangs loose against his chest and stomach, and his arms look strong and taut. He also seems totally comfortable with everyone staring at him.

Coach Elsberry smiles at him.

"Okay, people, Isabel and Josh will warm you up and set the pace. This is a slow two-mile run." He nods then says, Let's go. And stay together. Got it?" Coach claps his hands awkwardly, still holding his clipboard as Isabel begins counting and stretching her arms and legs. I follow along.

I guess I'm doing this.

"Come on, people. You're runners!" Coach shouts clapping his clipboard again. "Pretend you're enjoying yourselves."

We leave the field through a side gate at a slow shuffle, then trot down the long school driveway in clumps of twos and threes. My feet feel heavy. The air is humid and thick, and in a few minutes, I'm so drenched with sweat I could have been swimming. Some of the other kids are gasping for air or are red in the face. A few chat, making small talk. They all seem to know each other already.

Traffic whips by. I concentrate on my feet and putting one foot in front of the other. If Dad had come home, he would have made sure I was in shape, and there's no way that I would be huffing and puffing so badly now.

This is me, trying out. I can't imagine wearing all those football uniform pads in this heat. Running is hard enough.

How did you do it, Dad?

Why do I keep letting you down?

I keep my eyes on the pavement, sucking in air that's thick with the smell of French fries as we cross the sidewalk in front of the McDonald's. A truck belching smoke grinds its gears. The huge personnel transports on the base back home sounded exactly like that, every time a company left for overseas.

The pain in my throat makes it hard to breathe but I push myself, focusing on breathing, on my heart's thump in my chest. Before you know it, we're approaching the battlefield. Crooked fences line the edge of the woods leading up to the park's driveway.

I'm whupped and we're only halfway through. But, at least, I'm not the only one. Ahead, the sun bounces bright and sharp off the siding of the Battlefield Visitor's Center. Behind it, blue sky warns of another hot, windless day. There are no cars in the parking lot. It's too early for tourists. But there is a boy sitting on the wall staring across the Visitor's Center's parking lot.

No way!

I stop dead in my tracks.

Kids shout and gasp as they dodge me. Someone bumps my arm hard, but I don't take my eyes off the boy. A breeze stirs the edge of his shirt. He's wearing the same gray wool pants, muddy at the knees and streaked with grass stains.

Behind me someone shouts.

I spin around as Josh Gerber trots up. His eyebrows knit together. "What's wrong?" he asks, hands light on his hips as he stomps to a halt. "You need to rest?"

I turn back toward the Battlefield Boy. He's gone. Not like he walked away gone. More like he's completely nowhere-in-sight gone.

Disappeared.

Josh stares at me as if waiting for an explanation. Sweat drips from my face.

"Did you…?"

"Come on. Coach said to keep together," Josh moves past me. About ten feet down the sidewalk, he turns to see if I'm following him. I sprint to catch up, then stay a few steps behind him. He picks up speed.

I lower my eyes and match his pace. All I want right now is to get as far from that battlefield as possible.

JEREMY

"We're counting on you, Son." Pa said. "Your mother needs you here. I may be a Virginian, but I will not fight for slaveholders. You understand, don't you?"

The pale morning light washed the spring's colors into gray shadows. Even the sun seemed hesitant to rise that morning.

Pa was leaving, going north to join in the fight against slavery.

"Yes, sir." Jeremy looked away. Blue sniffed at Pa's blanket his tail wagging in the air.

Dang dog probably thought he'd be going with Pa, too. Yesterday they'd been planting fields. Today, Pa's skedaddling north and he's stuck at home with the women and old men. Doing chores. Anger gnawed at his gut.

He could shoot a Rebel as well as anyone. Ma said warring was a sin. Well, it seemed to him that sitting it out was worse.

"Old Man Carter will help out." Pa said. "He's too old to fight, and don't support the Secessionists neither." Pa was talking to Jeremy, but he was looking at Ma. "If I stay, they'll force me to muster with them. But those Rebels don't stand a chance against the United States Army. Everybody says so. I'll be back before you know it."

Pa's hand weighed Jeremy's shoulder down. The smell of dust and the woods rose from his pack. "I'm depending on you to keep this farm running, Jeremy. Fields don't tend themselves."

"Yes, sir."

"You take care of Annabelle and Ginny, now, you hear me?"

Jeremy nodded as Pa patted his shoulder, then shifted his hunting gun under his arm, and headed toward the woods behind the house. Blue trailed behind him.

"Blue, get back here. You ain't going." Blue stopped and turned toward Jeremy. Pa kept walking. The dog didn't budge.

"Blue!"

What was the matter with that dang animal?

The dog looked at Jeremy then back at Pa.

Now Jeremy's anger boiled over. "Blue, come!" Blue watched Pa walk away, then he returned to Jeremy's side. Jeremy didn't even bother to watch as Pa entered the woods. He trudged toward the barn. Somebody had to do the milking.

As he set the stool beside Annabelle, Blue settled in his usual spot facing out of the barn door. Ma approached the well outside the barn.

"I'll not have any sulking today, Jeremy." Her voice sounded sharp. "There's no time to feel sorry for yourself on a farm." Jeremy's heart dropped like a duck plugged with buckshot. Last night she called him a child. Well, 14 sure seemed old enough to fight Rebels. She could call soldiering a sin, but as far as he was concerned, if Lincoln needed him, he'd figure out a way to join the fight, and there was nothing Ma could do to stop him.

4

CHARLOTTE

THE FIRST DAY OF SCHOOL. I'M A WRECK. I DIDN'T SLEEP. At all. Thoughts of that kid nagged me all night, again. The image of him disappearing would not stop playing in my mind. It was like some meme on repeat.

On top of that, I'm about to walk into a school, named after some Confederate general I never even heard of, where I know nobody.

Talk about losers.

Kids flow by in a constant stream of laughter and chatter. No matter how much I try to smile and pretend I'm just like everyone else, it's a total lie. There is nothing normal about me. Somehow, I got to get through this day.

A quick look around confirms that absolutely no one is paying any attention to me. "Come on, C.C.! You got this!" I can just hear Dad clapping and pushing me through the doors.

He could do anything.

I force my way into the crush of kids going in the school's front doors. Far down at the end of the corridor a woman standing on a chair screams into a bullhorn. She says the same thing over and over, her voice droning with that weird bullhorn echo.

If I didn't know better, I would swear her voice was computer generated. No one is paying any attention to her, either.

"Eighth graders, pick up your schedules outside the main office. Seventh graders report to the auditorium."

"Okay, so where's the auditorium?"

"Follow the masses, dude, they know the way." A guy, with the longest eyelashes I've ever seen, says this and then disappears down the hall.

"Thanks," I say and dive into the flow of moving bodies. The current takes me around a corner and through a set of double doors.

In the auditorium kids are everywhere, perched on the edge of the stage, leaning against the wall, and clumped in groups in the aisles. Now it feels like everyone is staring at me, and they all know I'm new.

I search the rows of seats for a place to sit. About half-way down the aisle, a girl is twisting around in her seat waving to someone behind me. She's wearing a very tight tank top and sitting on the edge of the aisle seat squishing some guy into the arm rest. He dovesn't seem to care, though, he's got both his hands on her biceps like he's trying to keep her from falling into the aisle. I trudge down the auditorium steps.

"Alexis, Alexis, we saved you a seat," the girl says, patting the vacant seat behind her. She's obviously talking to someone else, but she's glaring at me, warning me off the seat I was about to take. I push past them, catching a whiff of Axe deodorant, and resist an urge to wrinkle my nose. It smells exactly like every young recruit my Dad brought home for dinner, the ones who looked like they could use a home-cooked meal.

I stomp the sting down hard, wishing I could pull the Battlefield Boy's trick. It would be so nice to disappear.

"Buck up, kid. Life takes courage" My father's voice inside my head says. "Be brave, Soldier."

Easy for him to say.

Shrugging off my backpack, I toss it onto a seat across the aisle as two adults plunge down the steps. They stop next to the girl and boy sharing the seat.

"I'm sorry, Miss. Please find a seat of your own. We have plenty," the man says. He seems unfazed by the pout she gives him, before she rolls her eyes, and swings a dark leather satchel over her shoulder.

"Fine, I'll sit with Alexis." Grabbing Alexis by the arm, and stomps up the aisle to the back of the auditorium. The man trots up the stairs to the stage. After a couple of seconds, he taps on the microphone at the podium.

"May I have your attention please?" Eventually, all other voices recede.

"Thank you," he says at last. "I'm Principal Phillips. I'd like to welcome you to Thomas Stonewall Jackson Middle School." With that he launches into what he calls Stonewall's FAQs. Somewhere between welcome to your new school, no smoking, vaping, "unauthorized" cell phone use, or hooking up on campus during school hours, I fade out. School around an army base meant you were always having to make new friends as the military moved you around. But everyone was in the same boat. Right now, I'd give anything to know one person.

With a glance at his watch, Mr. Phillips takes a deep breath, and nods at the adults at the back of the auditorium. "Okay," he says. "Let them in."

The entire 7th grade cranes their necks to turn around. The woman who had been directing traffic with the bullhorn in the lobby stands by the double doors at the top of the center aisle. She nods and pushes on the door latch. All three double doors release with a *clunk-crash.*

A wave of voices floods the room, and soon the auditorium is brimming with kids. Girls squeal and air-kiss people in the seats. Boys fist-bump their way down the aisles. Finally, everyone has a seat, and Mr. Philips taps the microphone again.

"May I have your attention please?" I swear he sounds exactly the same as he did earlier, like now *his* voice is a recording.

He delivers five whole minutes more of his speech when the doors at the rear of the auditorium crash open. Seats squeak as heads twists around again. In the doorway at the top of the center aisle, stands the boy with the long eyelashes who told me to follow the crowd. He scans the room wearing a huge grin that shows every tooth in his head. Some of the kids behind me bounce up and down in their seats nodding and clapping.

"Well, well, well," Mr. Phillips says. "I'm glad to see you decided to join us today, Mr. Finson."

"No problem, Mr. Phillips," the boy says as every eye watches him slouch down the aisle.

He gets about half-way down, then he waves his hand toward the stage and says, "Go on, go on." Laughter ripples through the crowd as he sits next to a couple of boys in baseball caps on backwards.

"It's nice to see you'll be picking up where you left off last spring, Eric," Mr. Phillips says. "I'll inform Mr. Burger you'll be joining him this afternoon for detention."

The boy sitting next to Eric extends his arms above his head. Eric turns grabs hold of his friend's hands and the two of them bob up and down in their seats, celebrating. The audience breaks into spontaneous applause. Mr. Phillips's face is calm. I can imagine what Dad would have said if he saw any of the kids from Base acting like that.

I am never going to fit in here.

Jeremy

May 23, 1861

The sound of drums outside the cabin startled Jeremy from a deep sleep. The same instant, Blue was up and barking. The full moon cast a bright swath of light across the floor. It was the middle of the night, still. What dang-blum fool was drumming at this hour? He'd likely raise the dead with all that noise.

Ma appeared at the door of her bedroom. A shawl grasped around her shoulders, she leaned forward, her head tilted to listen.

The drums sounded a long way off, but they grew louder by the second. Then another sound emerged through the dankness. Marching! Thousands of feet on the road across the pasture. Blue growled. Jeremy leaped out of bed toward his shot gun.

Now voices merged with the rhythm of the marching, a man shouting orders. That was no Virginian.

So, the North had come.

A low rumble sounded from deep in Blue's chest as he pointed his nose low at the cabin door. The dog barked and Ma jumped.

"Hush, Blue." Jeremy scolded. The dog whined and snapped his jaw closed, waiting for orders.

Pa had been gone for nearly a month. With all the talk of war, Jeremy and Ma kept to themselves as folks in town signed up to fight Lincoln. Day and night men marched by the house, nothing but a bunch of rowdies heading for a frolic. Not a one had a musket worth much, or even a uniform between them.

But these men, they were different. These men marched in perfect lines. Their uniforms pressed and clean.

This was a real army. Jeremy felt a thrill lift his chest.

Ma stood behind him. Row after row of men moving

steadily past their gate. Moonlight glinted off bayonets and now and again a shiny uniform button.

Now that Virginia had seceded, the Yanks were marching in.

Would Pa come back looking like these soldiers in a Union uniform like that? The thought raised a little flutter of excitement in Jeremy's chest. Pa was fighting for Lincoln.

Somehow, he had to get in it too.

"Thou shalt not kill," Ma said as if she had read his mind.

Jeremy's back tingled with dread. "Virginia doesn't aim to fight that army, does it… on account of the slaves?"

Ma looked at the endless stream of men pouring past the house. "May God have mercy on our souls," she whispered.

5

CHARLOTTE

TURNS OUT, THE CROSS-COUNTRY COACH, ALSO HAPPENS to be my World History teacher. He promised to post the team roster at the end of the first week of school. No one else is around when I check the list immediately before his class. With my head down, I sneak up to his office door.

With my heart jackhammering in my chest, I take a deep breath, close my eyes, and step closer to the paper.

"Cross, Charlotte" jumps off the page at me.

I exhale, then dash to class. As I slip in the door, Coach Elsberry gives me a wink and I take a seat at the back of the room. So far, he's an okay teacher. History has never been my thing, but he says if we want to know how the world got the way it is, we have to learn about the past. In Arizona, we learned about the desert and the mountains, and the people who lived there before we even were a country. Lots of those people still live there. Here, though, it seems to be all about wars. Old wars.

It's weird is all I'm saying.

The two girls I noticed at the opening day assembly are in this class, too. Ella, the girl who was sharing a seat with the boy in the auditorium, and Alexis, her best friend from elementary school, let me eat with them that awful first lunch. It turns out our schedules are identical.

The boy Ella was sitting with, whose name is Scott, is also in here. He's sitting at the back of the class with his hoodie pulled over his head. He's slumped low in the chair and might be asleep. He must think he's invisible or something. He's clearly not Coach's favorite student.

I settle into a seat next to Ella. Alexis is on her other side. I've moved around a lot, and making friends wasn't that hard when we lived on Base. Military kids hung out together. We all knew the rules. Friendships never lasted long because, sooner or later, someone moved.

Now, glancing at the only two people I know in the entire school, it hits me. This time, we're here to stay.

I know nothing about them, but they sure do know a lot of people. "I made the team," I say, not sure if they'll care.

"Of course, you did," Ella says. With her arms extended, she pats the front of our desks. "Now, we have some decisions to make about the weekend."

The new president, along with Stonewall Jackson, Thomas Jefferson, and George Washington all stare down from the wall behind us. The air conditioner kicks on. Ella lowers her voice.

"The Football team's first game is Saturday, and according to my sister, everybody goes." Ella squints at Alexis. "My sister says nobody actually watches the game, but we *have* to go." Neither Alexis nor I have an older brother or sister, which makes Ella the expert.

"You guys, let's meet at my house so we can get ready and go over together."

"Get ready for what?" I ask.

Ella squints at me sideways. "You know, get ready." She touches Alexis's shoulder.

"I know your mother absolutely forbids you from wearing makeup. But, Oh. My. God. I went nuts in Sephora at the beach last week. This girl at the store taught me how to use the black eyeliner. She said it made me look way older."

I'm not so sure about the makeup, but the football game might be fun. But before I have a chance to say anything, Coach Elsberry closes the door of the classroom and claps his hands once.

By the time the end of the class bell rings, I'm feeling antsy. As we're packing up, Coach calls me over to his desk. I watch Alexis and Ella head out.

"I'm happy to have you on the team, Charlotte," he says.

I mumble a thank you and look at my feet. "Ya know," he continues, "I went to high school with your dad." A shock wave crashes through me to my toes.

"You knew my dad?"

"Yep. I was a year behind him in school. He was quite the athlete," Coach says. "I'll never forget watching him dodge tacklers and running full out. He scored touch downs like there was no stopping him." He smiles. "I hope we'll be able to coax some of that famous Cross speed out of you."

I nod. I guess I should have known someone would remember him.

"To be honest, we all were devastated by the news. I'm sorry for your loss." He stops talking like he's afraid to say anything else.

"Yeah," I say. Most people expect you to smile and nod when they say they're sorry. I don't know why people say it in the first place. It's so stupid. Like anything they say can make a difference.

"You better go," he says, "The next bell's about to ring."

I hurry out the door. It's because of football that Dad got recruited to play for State. To pay for it, he did ROTC. That's how he ended up in the Army. And sent to Afghanistan.

And we know how that turned out.

Jeremy

May 24, 1861

The scraping of heavy boots on the porch step startled Jeremy awake. He and Blue sat outside all night in the rocking chair on the front porch. With his gun across his knees, Jeremy felt like he was watching a parade. Row after row of marching men didn't stop the whole night. Now, as the sun reflected orange on the clouds, a genuine officer of the United States Army was standing right there in front of him.

Blue sat alert by Jeremy's feet. The Union officer, lean and straight, stared at them, his head so high that Jeremy could see clear up his nose. Two more officers stood behind the first one in the dirt.

Jeremy scrambled to his feet and leaned his gun against his shoulder, pointing it straight up like he had seen the soldiers do the night before. He puffed his chest out.

"Well, well, this must be Jeremy."

How did this Yankee know his name?

"Charles?" Ma's voice, raised in surprise, called from inside the cabin. She appeared at the front door, her eyebrows high. "Why, it is thee," Ma said wiping her hands on her apron.

Charles? Jeremy squinted as the officer climbed the last steps, took Ma's hand, and bowed.

Uncle Charles? Pa's brother.

Jeremy hadn't seen his Uncle Charles since he had passed through Washington on his way west with the Cavalry of the United States Army. Now he'd come back with President Lincoln's troops. Jeremy trembled he was so excited.

"I can't believe it. Charles! Mother Turner never said a word about thee in her letters." Jeremy squinted at Ma. She usually only used thee and thou with other members of the Quaker Meeting. It sounded so formal.

"I apologize, Laurie. Mother didn't know. Regimental movements are generally kept secret, even from one's mother." The Yankee officer smiled. He turned toward Jeremy and Ma followed his gaze.

"Jeremy, put down that gun." Ma sounded embarrassed but stiff. "Mind your manners. Come here and shake thy uncle's hand. One would think thee were raised in the barn," she scolded. He relaxed and lowered the gun to his side. Charles extended his hand and Jeremy shook it, eyeing the other men behind his tall uncle.

Had they seen his hands trembling? Would they think he was a coward?

"He's grown so tall, Laurie. He's the image of John."

"Is he? I think he rather favors my father. But my recollection of him has faded some. Too painful to think about. How are thy parents, Charles? Thy mother's letters are fewer and fewer these days.

Ma noticed the men behind Charles. Uncle Charles turned to the men still on the dirt. "Where are my manners?" He stepped back. "Laurie…" He stopped. "Mrs. John Turner, may I present my two lieutenants, Thorton Walker." The man with the tight red beard bowed and said, "Mrs. Turner." Ma nodded her head. "Very pleased to meet thee, Lieutenant."

"And James McPherson." Now the taller of the two bowed. "Charmed, Mrs. Turner."

"I'd be pleased to offer thee a cup of coffee," Ma said. "I have a pot on to boil. It should be ready any minute."

"I'm very sorry to barge in on you this way, Laurie. This is the first chance I've had to ride over to see you since we've returned from California.

My regiment will be in the vicinity indefinitely. We've been assigned the defense of Washington."

"The defense of Washington?" Ma gasped. "Charles, surely President Lincoln does not expect Virginia to attack the capital?" Ma laid her hands on her heart. "My word! What has begun?"

"I'm afraid I cannot say what the President thinks Virginia will do. But I have my orders." He smiled at Ma. "But enough of this unseemly discussion. We'd be pleased to join you for a cup of coffee. It's been much too long since I've heard any news from you or John. Mother informs me that he's gone north. Lincoln can use as many good men as he can get."

Ma's mouth went flat. Jeremy wondered if these Union officers knew what kind of danger they were headed into having coffee with Ma. He walked toward the barn, his heart rapping against the inside of his chest like a rabbit scratching an ear. He was burning to listen to Uncle Charles talk about soldiering, but knew better than to put off chores.

To think, Uncle Charles, a genuine officer in the United States Cavalry, was sitting in his home. He'd been out West fighting Indians. If he got through all the work, maybe he could listen through the window.

Not even Ma can stop ears from hearing.

6

CHARLOTTE

THAT AFTERNOON AT PRACTICE, COACH ELSBERRY GATHERS us all in the infield. The freshly painted twenty-yard line of the football field serves as our gathering point.

"We'll meet right here every day," Coach says. "But if the football team catches us puny runners out here on their turf, our side won't stand a gnat's chance in a bug zapping factory. So, my goal, as your coach, is to move you out of here before they take the field. All those pads take a long time to put on. One more reason to love running. All you need is a pair of shoes. Okay, and some legs." Some of the kids nod and laugh. The 8th graders shake their heads. I guess they've heard the joke before.

Being on the team feels good. But I'm not nearly as ready as I should be.

I stifle the sting of letting Dad down.

Coach is going over the school's grade requirements for participation in sports. Most teams will let you play if you have a B. Coach Ellsbury has a different standard. For his runners, "Anything below a B+ in any class will keep you out of meets, no matter how fast your times."

Coach looks around the group. "No dumb jocks on the

running team. Got it?" We nod. A couple of kids shout, "Yes, sir, Coach," like army recruits.

"So, with that in mind," Coach continues, "We have a buddy system. Each 7th grader gets an 8th grade mentor whose job it is to keep you from falling behind. You'll meet your bud-dy twice a week. "If you have to read MacBeth-- your buddy will help you make sense out of it. If your lousy, son-of-a-gun history teacher assigns a research topic," he catches my eye and winks, "let your buddy know. They will help you stay on track." He makes air quotes.

A couple of kids laugh.

While he reads out each 7th graders' names and who their buddies are, I kick the grass of the infield with the toe of my shoe.

"Cross, Charlotte…" My heart jumps at the sound of my name. Coach pauses and then looks up at me. "With a name like that, seems like you were born to run Cross-Country."

My father called me C.C. I never really thought about it before. Maybe that's why?

Coach looks at me. "Isabel Price is your partner." I look at Isabel and my breathing stops. Isabel pulls on her toe, stretching her quad. One hand rests on Josh Gerber's shoulder. She smiles at me. Josh nods and smiles, too. I look away fast. Every time I've seen Josh since our little jog from the Battlefield, he's been with Isabel, and I wish again, for the millionth time that, somehow, someway, I can learn the Battlefield Boy's disappearing trick.

I don't hear what Coach says after that except that we're doing stairs.

As the older kids groan, I take a deep breath. I hadn't realized that I was holding it. Since we're staying on campus, there's no chance of running into the disappearing boy. I start my first trip to the top of the bleachers, grateful for the distraction. For a second it hits me. Was it the stairs, or thoughts of the Battlefield Boy causing my heart to race.

Or maybe it's Josh.

Jeremy

Jeremy washed his hands at the well. The freezing water stung his fingers.

He filled Blue's water bowl. Where was that dog? He hadn't seen him all morning. The three Cavalry officers' horses stood in the shade, just where they had left them, their reins trailing in the dirt. Still saddled and switching their tails, they hadn't moved. Jeremy had never known of a horse who didn't wander when it was loose.

He walked toward the tall bay, rubbed the mare's neck then patted her rump. She stood straight but showed no skittishness or fear. What a beauty. The other two animals, a roan and a broad-chested grey, seemed equally handsome. And equally well trained. The US Cavalry would make short work of the

Rebels. Pa would be home in no time. Something leaden shifted in his chest. It'll be over before he even has a chance to join up.

When Jeremy entered the cabin, all talk stopped. The smell of freshly brewed coffee filled the room. The three men sat at their small rough, wooden table, making the front room feel cramped.

Sitting straight in their chairs, the Yankee officers held their coffee cups in front of them like they were having tea in some fancy city parlor. Ma's back was stiff and formal. She didn't like entertaining these military men. That was clear.

Blue sat at one of the officers' feet. The man rubbed the dog's back with a strong, steady stroke. Blue's eyes were closed.

At the sight of Jeremy, the red-bearded officer stood abruptly, his chair squealing on the wood floor. "Mrs. Turner, it has been most kind of you to share your morning coffee with us.

Now, I am afraid we must be returning to our regiment."

"Thorton, you do worry," Uncle Charles said. He turned to Ma. "Lieutenant Walker is better than a pocket watch for keeping me on schedule. If he says it's time to be getting back, I know better than to contradict him."

The other officer stood and bowed to Ma. Blue snapped out of his trance. Ma lowered her eyes. "I'll help Lieutenant Walker with the horses," he said. "I thank you kindly, ma'am, for the pleasure of your company. And the delicious coffee. Army rations, especially on the march, rarely satisfy." He bowed. "Your hospitality has reminded me of my own wife's kitchen. I am grateful to you for that."

Blue followed the man to the cabin door and Jeremy moved to the hearth. His fingers hadn't thawed from his overnight outside. The fire warmed his face as he poured himself a cup of coffee. Its warmth spread through him as he swallowed a mouthful.

Uncle Charles stood and followed his men.

They're leaving? He hadn't heard a lick of war news.

It was her. She wanted to keep him from listening. He hurried to the door behind Uncle Charles.

Outside his uncle touched his hat and bent slightly at the waist. Ma bowed her head..

"I'll send word to Mother that I saw you," he said. "She has been very anxious for you since John wrote. She will be pleased to hear your news. And I'll be sure to tell her how tall and strong Jeremy has grown. She does worry, I'm afraid." Despite the sun's warmth on the porch, and Uncle Charles's charm, Jeremy had never seen Ma look so cold. She did not like these men wearing their swords on their belts and coming into her home. She was a Quaker still, even though they wouldn't have her in a Meeting. Dang peace testimony. It sure seems like a lot of wasted words now that Virginia was fighting to keep their slaves.

"I'll listen for news of John," Uncle Charles said. "I know the officers in some of the Pennsylvania Regiments. We'll find him, Laurie. Don't worry." Uncle Charles glanced at Jeremy.

A rush of heat surged through him. They had been talking about Pa.

"Have you seen him, sir? Do you know where he is?" Jeremy knew his mother would give him an earful for interrupting, but he had to ask. "I can shoot as straight as anyone, sir. Do you think they'll let me join up?"

"Jeremy!" Ma gasped.

Uncle Charles smiled and gave Jeremy's hand a quick shake. "I'm afraid I can't answer any of those questions, my boy," Uncle Charles said. "But you leave the fighting to the men. We'll have this business over soon enough. In the meantime, your family needs you here. You take care of your mother. A farm is a lot of work."

A searing lump in his stomach pulsed. He ain't no boy. He could fight, no matter what Ma and her Quakers had to say about it.

Uncle Charles turned back to Ma. "Don't worry about a thing, Laurie," he said. "I'll post sentries on the lane to your property. No one will bother you under orders from me." Now Jeremy's anger boiled. Dang right, no one would bother them. His hunting gun would see to it.

"I thank thee, Charles," Ma managed a weak smile. "You are family. You are welcome in our home." Jeremy wondered if Uncle Charles knew that was the one and only reason she had allowed them in. "Goodbye now," she said and hurried back inside, her spine straight as a broomstick. She was good and angry. Jeremy didn't even have to see her face to know she had not approved of all the talk of war. Or of his interrupting.

Jeremy watched Uncle Charles trot down the road on the

lithe bay. "Come in and eat your biscuits, Jeremy." Ma's voice was terse and clipped. "There's still hours of chores to do."

7

CHARLOTTE

HEAT SHIMMERS ABOVE THE SCHOOL'S DRIVEWAY AS I start for home after practice. We finished later than usual. It was a hard workout. My legs feel like rubber.

Ella and Alexis said they would wait for me, but there's no sign of them. Not even a text.

It's fine. Scott Osborne had probably shown up. He introduced them to a whole group of guys. They probably got distracted.

Car horns and diesel fumes make me cringe as I start up Richelieu. Back in Arizona, there was always someone to walk with back to base. Sometimes, when he was between deploy-ments, Dad met me at school to walk me home.

I turn up Ashton Parkway, cross and turn into a newer housing development. I reach the end of the first block and cut toward the far end of the neighborhood, the part where the houses are older and not all alike.

On the other side of the road, a stand of pines hides an industrial park that borders the Battlefield. A gust of wind sweeps across the street, and the branches lining the curb start rolling crazily.

Funny. It doesn't look like it's about to rain.

Then I freeze. Standing at the curb across the street is the Battlefield Boy. I have no idea why people say their heart stops when something scares them. Mine is kicking up a storm.

He's just standing there, staring at me.

Cars roar between us. Without taking his eyes off me, the boy steps into the street. A pickup truck barrels past. He doesn't flinch.

I glance both ways. "Wait!" I shout.

In the gap between a van and a motorcycle, he steps across the white line marking the curb lane.

"No!" I scream. "You're gonna get hit!"

Cars speed toward us from both directions. I cover my eyes. When I look again, he's at the line in the middle of the street but the traffic isn't slowing.

He takes another step.

"Stop!" my voice grates against my throat. It's like the cars don't even see him—like he's not even there.

The guttural engine of a garbage truck grows louder, closer. I clap my hands over my ears and squeeze my eyes shut.

There's no squeal of tires, no thud of a body hitting metal. Only the hiss of wheels on asphalt, car radios, and the rush of hot air. I open my eyes and gasp. The boy steps up onto the curb two feet in front of me. An ache spreads from my chest to my face as tears pool in my eyes. My knees are shaking.

Then that stupid lock of hair falls across the boy's face, and he smiles at me. "Where's Blue?" he says as if we were meeting in the hallway at school.

"Who are you?" I ask. My voice breaks.

"I'm Jeremy," he says. "Not Thaddeus."

"Jeremy?" I'm distracted by the stupid twig that's been dangling from the back of his head since I first saw him. Without thinking, I raise my hand to grab it. Then, suddenly, I'm standing alone on the sidewalk, the twig, pinched between my finger and thumb.

I feel like I've been hit by a truck.

Jeremy

June 18, 1861

Dust rose from Blue's paws as Jeremy trudged behind him along the road that marked the end of Old Man Carter's pasture. A gentle movement at the tips of the grass by the side of the road hinted of a breeze. He clipped the end off a tall blade within reach. No amount of wind could help in this kind of heat. The buzzing crescendo of a cicada rattled the stillness, then faded. Even the bugs seemed lazy today.

Ma would be angrier than a hornet in a pickle jar if she found out where Jeremy was going. As far as he was con-cerned, she would never find out that he had so much as crossed the creek.

Up until now, it seemed like nobody had even fired a shot in this war. There sure had been some kind of dust-up yesterday, though. And from the sound of it and the smell of gunpowder in the air this morning, it had been close by.

Last night, the sky flashed yellow and orange like lightning coming out of the ground, the guns sounded like corn popping on the fire.

The battle had been over quickly, and they never got close to the cabin. But it was a battle, alright. With his hunting gun charged and ready, Jeremy squinted out the window. Blue sat next to him trembling. Pa had trained Blue well. He didn't make a peep when he saw that gun. Just let one no-good Rebel show up on his land, and they'd find out fast that even Quakers know how to defend themselves.

Ma sat in the rocker, praying and rocking the whole time those boys were shooting at each other. The next morning, smoke from the shooting lingered in the air like fog.

Now as he and Blue trotted down the lane toward where the ruckus had been, Jeremy grumbled about Ma. "She has no cause to be angry at a body for having a look." Blue's tongue lolled out the side of his mouth.

"I want to see what all the commotion was about. One thing's for sure. There's always going to be farm work to do. You never know when those boys'll be fighting so close again."

Jeremy walked for some minutes in silence. Thirst scraped

at his throat., and the sun felt like it would drill a hole into his brain. Sweat trickled down his neck and back. Blue panted.

"It's so dang hot," Jeremy said. "Maybe that's why Ma's so sleepy lately. Maybe she can't stand the heat?" Blue's pace didn't change.

Lately Ma slept in the rocker in the middle of the afternoon, her head thrown back and her mouth open. And every morning Ma dragged herself out of bed, hurrying out the door of the cabin to throw up in the dirt. Jeremy didn't want her to know that he heard her retching. Fear crawled up his spine. With both armies so close, everybody he knew had fled, either further west or to Richmond. He wasn't sure if Doc Crosby was still in town or if he had packed up, too. He'd better check on his next trip into town in case Ma was sick or something.

He didn't know anything about tending sick folks. Would he have to do the women's work too, on top of all the farm work? He tossed the piece of grass he had been toying with and swore.

Jeremy and Blue crept along the roadbed, following the railroad line from Alexandria. For a long time, they didn't see anything but horse dung and flies. Then the ground changed. Holes the size of cows spread in front of him, their rims charred black. Jeremy slipped in the loose dirt and rolled into the ditch at the side of the road. As he scrambled out the wind kicked up. A stench, thick as smoke, came from over the next rise. Blue's nose went up. He sniffed the air in quick bursts, then he dashed ahead.

"Blue, ya crazy dog. Where're you going?" Jeremy chased Blue a few steps then stopped like he'd reached the end of a tether. In a ditch ten feet in front of him lay the bloated carcass of a dead horse. Guts spilled from its split belly and caked blood stained the dirt around it. A black cloud hung over the animal, accompanied by a loud humming – the buzzing of millions of flies.

"Yeoow!" Jeremy yelled as his stomach flipped upside down. He covered his nose and mouth. He could taste it!

Don't breathe.

He needed to lie down. He bent over with his hands on his knees, then mustered his strength. The stench wormed its way into his nose and throat, choking him.

His stomach roiling, Jeremy mustered his voice. "Get back here, Blue. Get back here this instant."

The dog returned to Jeremy's side. Gravel and dirt slipped as Jeremy stumbled, clawing his way up the embankment at the side of the road. Jeremy didn't dare take another glimpse at the horse. With shaking knees, he gasped for air. Tears filled his eyes, his stomach lurched, and he threw up.

8

CHARLOTTE

SLEEPING THAT NIGHT WAS NOT AN OPTION.

Whatever happened on the street this afternoon, I cannot stop playing over and over through my brain.

He said his name was Jeremy, not Thaddeus, then…

I am not hallucinating. I did not make it up. The twig is sitting right there, on my bedside table.

Around 3:30 am, I give up and stop pretending I'm going to fall asleep. Dad's laptop whirs to life.

The Internet is my only hope.

The fi rst search, "Jeremy Ma nassas Ba ttlefield Vir ginia" brings up pages and pages of pages of Jeremys who live near Manassas, but most of them are social media profiles that don't look anything like my Battlefield Boy.

I should have guessed it wouldn't be that easy.

The next search, "Jeremy," "Manassas," and "disappearing" is not much better. There's a story about a disappearing stand of hemlock trees that have been affected by some invading bug, written by a guy named Jeremy for the Manassas Guardian. And a story about Jeremy Johns, the celebrity that kids from Manassas were trying to invite to their graduation.

He's from Virginia or something.

This isn't working. I rest my head on my hands at the edge of the keyboard. It's useless. Then I straighten up and add "Black Lab," to the search bar.

That does it. I scroll through the first few hits and one word screams out at me: "ghost." Goosebumps crawl up my arms and neck as I scroll through link after link of "Black Lab" paired with "Ghost" and "Manassas Battlefield."

I click on a YouTube video: "Not even the grave can stop a boy from searching for his dog."

The opening music for the local TV news blares from my speakers. I smash the mute button. It looks like some kind of Halloween story from a couple of years ago, complete with lightning-flash special effects and a reporter dressed in a Sherlock Holmes costume.

I jab my earphones in the jack as an image of the battlefield shrouded in mist resolves to black on my screen. A narrator asks, "Do you believe in ghosts? Well, this story is guaranteed to make even the biggest of skeptics think again."

The scene shifts to a view of the Stonewall statue on the battlefield. There's a dog, a black lab, running in slow motion around the base. Off to the side is a group of kids reading the same sign I read on my fist run at Manassas.

The narrator continues. "Most people when asked will tell you they don't believe in ghosts. Others say they aren't sure. But residents of Manassas, Virginia are finding it pretty hard to explain recent events at their town's famous battlefield."

The scene shifts again, this time to a reporter talking to a guy in a camo jacket and boots, with a big beard.

"Meet Clay Brewster. This former Army Special Operations Officer took his family to pay their respects to the fallen soldiers of Manassas Battlefield this afternoon when something out of the ordinary occurred that has park rangers scratching their heads, but local residents nodding in recognition. Retired Army Major Brewster says that he and his family, along with their black Labrador, Dexter, were enjoying the park earlier today when a young man, who seemed to be dressed as a Civil War re-enactor approached the dog." The camera focuses on the black dog panting at its owner's side.

"This kid came up to Dexter here, bent down and started hugging him like they'd know each other their whole lives." Dexter's owner scratches at the back of his neck. "My dog is real friendly, and he loves people, so I stood back and let him enjoy the attention."

The camera returns to the reporter. "Then what happened?'" The camera switches again to the man who seems embarrassed to say what happened next. But I know exactly what's coming.

"Well, I honestly can't explain it, but I walked up to the guy, introduced myself and before I could get my whole name out..." He stops and squints at the camera.

"It's okay, Sir. Please, tell us what happened and let our viewers draw their own conclusions," the reporter says.

"Well, the kid…he…disappeared. He was just gone. Poof."

A woman appears on the screen next. "The kids and I were reading that sign over there. Out of the corner of my eye I saw a kid approach Dexter. I didn't think much of it. He's a very friendly dog. When I looked back my husband was standing there but there was no sign of the boy. Dexter was sniffing the ground like he was following a scent, but he was basically going in circles."

The camera returns to the man, who says, "It was pretty freaky, actually." Then a little girl talking into the camera with a microphone in her face, "I think it's cool. Maybe he's a ghost who lost his dog."

The scene shifts again to a mist-filled night shot with a full moon and the statue of the general in the foreground. The reporter says, "We contacted the National Park Service for more information. Here is what Officer Peter Vanderly said when asked about the boy, and please note, in my question, I do not speculate about paranormal activity at the park." A scratchy recording of a phone call plays. "Officer Vanderly, we've had a report of a boy on the battlefield searching for a dog. Can you explain to our viewers what the Park Service might know about that?"

After a short pause, the officer says, "I won't confirm or deny incidents of supernatural or paranormal phenomena occurring on park grounds.

"The best I can tell you is that folks who come to the park with a black Labrador have reported meeting a boy who matches the description you've given me. They all claim that he vanishes without a trace, right before their eyes."

The reporter says, "There you have it, folks. Is the vanishing boy a ghost? I, for one, will not speculate. But if you are up for a real haunting experience this Halloween, you might want to bring your dog on over to the Manassas Battlefield Park and see who turns up.

"Back to you, Rachel."

I hit the pause button on the video and glance at the twig sitting on my bed-side table. It glows blue in the light from a streetlamp outside my window.

Jeremy is real. Now what?

JEREMY

June 18, 1861

Uncle Charles had not been back, but for days Union soldiers poured past the farm. Lincoln's army and their tents were everywhere, in fields, on pastures, in town. They swarmed over the county like bees in a hive. Poor Blue was hoarse from barking at the line of soldiers marching on the road. Jeremy tied

Blue up behind the house so he wouldn't chase them. He had better things to do than worry about what that dog was up to.

After one column of soldiers marched straight across his field, destroying the crop Jeremy and Pa planted, another bunch of them camped there overnight. Jeremy surveyed the mess of mud, charred wood, and slop.

Now Ginny was hitched to the plow, again. Poor girl. She was getting too old to be doing this field for a second time. But he had no choice.

Blue watched from his post under the oak tree as Jeremy and Ginny crossed the field at a dead slow walk.

Halfway through the middle rows a sound over the next hill caught Jeremy's attention — the low rumble of a horse cantering. Ginny must have known he wasn't paying attention. She stopped and flicked her tail across her back. Foam dripped from her back.

A rider wearing a Union officer's uniform crested the hill beyond the pasture. More men in Union uniforms followed close behind him on foot. Four across, they streamed past in what seemed like an endless line of blue. Jeremy glanced at his dog resting under the tree. He'd wear himself out from barking.

That army sure was a sight to see, though. That was a real army, not the raggedy gaggle of Virginians who thought they could take on the United States Army. His whole body burned. He could be fighting with Pa.

If it weren't for Ma.

Jeremy's shoulders slumped. Then he flicked Ginny's reins and clicked his tongue. "Come on, girl. We only got a few more rows." But the horse didn't budge. She raised her head and shook it in protest. She could see the men and hear their marching as well as he could. She knew that sooner or later, they would tromp across this newly plowed field, like they did the last one. He didn't have the heart to push her. It was too dang hot.

"I know it, girl," he said out loud as if she had been talking to him "We can take a break. You've done about all you can for the day, I expect."

Jeremy glanced toward the column of soldiers on the road as he walked toward Ginny's head. An officer broke away from the line of men and trotted toward him. Three more horsemen followed, stomping on Jeremy's carefully plowed rows.

Ginny blew air out of her nose and her body deflated. There goes that morning's work.

Jeremy's heart kicked at his ribs as the men rode steadily toward him. Blue was barking, raspy and urgent, as he strained at the end of his lead.

Ma stepped out onto the cabin's porch. She shaded her eyes, watching the approaching horseman, too.

The men pulled their horses up, spraying Jeremy with dirt. He squinted up at the man in the front.

"I have orders to confiscate your horse," the officer said as his horse danced. "One of our artillery mules has come up lame. Please drop the reins and step back. These men will unhitch the animal."

Jeremy's face grew hot.

"You can't take my horse." Jeremy stepped between the horsemen and Ginny.

"That was not a request, young man. We need your horse. I will give you a receipt for reimbursement. Now, step aside. We don't want to hurt you or the animal."

The man signaled to his men, and they dismounted. Ginny neighed as if she knew they were arguing about her.

"I said, you can't take my horse," Jeremy repeated. "I have a field to plow. The army destroyed the last crop I put in."

"Well look–y here, fellas." One of the men on the ground said, his high-pitched voice twanged with a strange accent. "One of these Rebels has a backbone. That will make taking his horse that much more enjoyable."

As the men moved to surround him, Jeremy stared at the officer still on horseback. "I am no Rebel," he said to the officer. "My father is fighting in Pennsylvania. My Uncle is—"

Jeremy doubled over. Light flashed as Blue's raspy bark drifted through the fog in his head.

Bile burned his throat. Ginny whinnied.

They had sucker punched him.

They will not take her.

Gasping for air, he seized the fury in his gut and came up swinging.

"I am no Rebel."

Before his fist connected, the two men were on him, dragging him away from the third. Jeremy twisted, tugging his arms and kicking at the men holding him. All three toppled into the dirt, one on top of him and the other underneath. Jeremy squirmed free and climbed to his knees just as the man who had punched him pulled Jeremy's head back by the hair and pressed a pistol to Jeremy's temple. The cold metal smelled of powder and gun oil.

Jeremy's throat constricted with the weight of the man's hand pulling on his head. He couldn't breathe. Needles of pain tore at the roots of his hair. The other two men scrambled to their feet and drew their weapons. Rage surged through Jeremy as he lifted his hands away from his sides.

"Sergeant Taylor, that's enough!" the officer on horseback shouted. "Our orders were to confiscate the horse, not to kill the boy." His voice was calm, now.

He addressed Jeremy. "Young man, these two men are going to unhitch your horse, while Sergeant Taylor, here, ensures that you do not interfere. You will receive a receipt for the animal which you can present to the district Disbursement officer for payment. Is that clear?"

Jeremy didn't answer. If they aimed to take Ginny, he would not give her up without a fight. "Is that clear, boy?"

"Colonel Grimsby." A fifth man cantered across Jeremy's newly plowed field. "Colonel Grimsby, Sir." The horse stopped abruptly sending up a shower of pebbles and mud.

The Colonel turned in his saddle to see who approached. The two men saluted as the newcomer came close.

"Major Thomas has secured an animal further up the line, sir. He said you should return at once to oversee the switch."

Grimsby turned to Jeremy. "It would appear your horse is no longer needed. You are free to finish your field."

Jeremy seethed.

They had no right.

"Release him, Sergeant Taylor. Even a rebel with backbone is smart enough to count his blessings and cause no more trouble. Isn't that right, son?"

Taylor pushed Jeremy from behind with his foot in the middle of his back at the same time that he released his hair. His teeth and face hit the muck. He tasted mud.

Jeremy scrambled to his feet, spitting dirt. His shirt and pants, soaked with red clay, stuck to his legs and chest. He touched the back of his hand to his mouth. A smear of blood mixed with the grime.

"That animal wouldn't have lasted the day anyway, Colonel," one of the men said as they mounted to leave. "Worthless Rebel horseflesh."

"I ain't no Rebel!" he shouted at their backs.

Jeremy stumbled toward Ginny and patted her rump to calm her.

"It's over, girl. Don't worry. They're gone." He walked behind her, straightened the plow and unhitched it.

"I'd say you've had enough excitement for one day. How about some water and a good rub down." Jeremy watched Lincoln's army march by. Ma moved toward him across the field behind Blue, her skirt dragging in the mud.

Bastards!

The next time anyone of them sets foot on his land, he didn't care whose army they were in. They'd see what he was made of.

9

CHARLOTTE

I DIDN'T SLEEP THE WHOLE NIGHT, BUT SOMEHOW, I manage to pull myself together the next morning and show up at Ella's on time. Every time I started to drift off, Jeremy walked through a wall of speeding cars all over again, and I jolted awake. Then it was the YouTube video that played on repeat in my head.

But what kept me awake was something else. If Jeremy is a ghost, it they really exist, what about Dad?

Could he be wandering a roadside in Afghanistan somewhere? Could he be trying to get home?

To me?

I bump right into Alexis when she stops at the entrance to the track to survey the crowd.

Her lip curls up and she squints at me. "Sorry," I say and back off.

Right now, this whole pretending-to-care-about-the-game thing feels…stupid. My mind is a million miles away and I'm sitting at a football game that I don't even care about.

On the field, a marching band plays some fight song that sounds vaguely familiar. A few people in the stands are singing along. Ella and Alexis stand at the gate that leads to the stands like they're waiting for their cue to walk the runway. In their tight jeans, spaghetti strap tops, and eyeliner, they seem way older than 13.

I watch Ella as she scans the crowd. In a millisecond her face goes from mildly bored to a quick confident smile, then back to bored. I follow her glance and see why. Scott Osborne is heading our way. He swaggers over like he's got nothing better to do. Like it's no big deal for him to come say "Hi." His eyes never sway from Ella, and it's so clear that she knows it, even though she's looking in the opposite direction. She pulls her hair over her shoulder.

Alexis glances at me and lifts an eyebrow. She chuckles under her breath. She obviously saw this coming.

Behind Scott, there's another kid I've seen around. I think his name is Tyler. He's in my math class. They stroll up, but neither of them smiles. There's an uneven slant to Scott's mouth as he points at Tyler and then at Ella and Alexis, who smile and wave their hands together as if they've practiced the move. I can't hear what anyone is saying because the band is so loud. I expect Scott or Tyler to nod at me, next, or at least to acknowledge I'm there. Something. Anything. But nope. Neither of them even looks at me. My face burns. Apparently, I'm invisible. Tyler leans over to say something into Alexis's ear, and she smiles and nods. Scott and Ella lead us up the stands to a spot at the top.

We sit there for what can only be five minutes when Ella and Scott lose interest in the game. Ella stands up, stretches with her hands over her head like she's been sitting there for hours. The hem of her shirt rides up revealing a skinny tanned waist. Scott's eyes travel the full length of her body. I turn away. It's embarrassing how he's looking at her.

The band drowns out everything but the whistles of the refs on the field, so talking is out of the questions. Not that anyone has anything to say to me. I don't care. I am so dead from not sleeping, I swear I could curl up right here, and nod off, even with the band blaring off-key horns in my ear.

Alexis is turned away from Ella, so she misses the cue to move. She's laughing as Tyler shouts something into her ear. Then Tyler grabs her elbow and they're standing up, too. Alexis signals for me to follow her, and the next thing I know we're all heading down the stairs to the track again. I follow even though I don't have a clue what's happening. At the bottom, Alexis, shouts in my ear, "We're getting something to eat."

I nod.

Tyler leads us toward the white trailer that's the food stand at the entrance to the field.

There's a long line of people, all wearing Stonewall Football t-shirts and jerseys, waiting to buy food. Instead of getting in the back of the line, Scott signals for us to follow Tyler. We cut behind the trailer, step over thick black cords, and head toward the gym entrance to the school. My stomach growls at the smell of cooking hot dogs. As we round the corner of the building, the sound of the band and the crowd is muffled.

"Where're we going?" I ask. "I thought we were getting hot dogs."

"Tyler's neighbor is in charge of concessions, so we don't have to wait in line," Alexis says.

We approach the back entrance to the gym. The cords that lead to the trailer keep the door to the gym from closing. Tyler pulls it open.

I don't like this.

Our sneakers squeal on the polished wood floor as we cross the basketball court. A tsunami of signals go off in my brain when Tyler presses his back against the wall and peeks out the gym door to the hallway. Suddenly I can't breathe.

"Should we be in here?" I ask.

Alexis's face is lit up like she's about to get a huge birthday present. "We're not doing anything," she says, and my heart drops right through the gym floor.

"Not yet we're not." Tyler says. My whole body screams to turn around and run, but I follow them as we creep down the hall.

Sucking in his breath, Tyler steps around the corner.

We shouldn't be here.

With his back to the wall Scott sneaks a look over his shoulder through the vertical window on the door of the Sports Department closet at the end of the hall. Then he pushes the door open. Tyler takes out his cell phone and shines the flash-light inside. It reveals shelves and shelves of boxes of Twix bars, Snickers, Hershey bars, Oreo cookies, sour gummy worms, Doritos, and chips. On the floor sit crates of Sprite, Coke, and bottles of water. Alexis giggles. She's nervous. Not me. I'm panicking.

"They never lock these doors during the game," Tyler says." It's too much trouble keeping track of a key. Which means…" He pauses as he takes a boxful of snickers and a carton of chips. "We can bypass the middleman."

"I don't know, you guys," I say. Just then, the door to the gym crashes against the wall. "Come on!" Tyler whispers, and he bursts out the door, and runs in the opposite direction of the door we came in. Scott, Ella, Alexis, and I take off behind him. With all the adrenaline surging through me, I sprint past them all. I cut around a corner and wait, panting. In a second, they slide to a stop and throw themselves against the wall next to me. Scott's holding a carton of chips in one hand and Ella's hand in the other. Alexis and Ella both have a box of candy bars. They're gasping and trying to stifle their laughter.

"We could have been caught, you guys," I say, my voice rising in a high-pitched whisper.

"Yeah," Tyler says as he pushes himself off the wall and heads toward the door to the school's parking lot. "But we weren't." He breaks open the box of Snickers and hands Alexis one.

She rips the wrapper with her teeth then takes a huge bite. She's smiling like she's never had so much fun in her life.

I'm shaking so hard I'm amazed I can walk.

We hurry off school grounds without anyone stopping us. I guess no one is interested in the game anymore. My heart is up in my throat, which is so tight I have to force myself not to cry.

Stupid! Stupid! Stupid!

In the back of my mind, I hear Dad's voice. "Honor. Duty. Courage. At the end of the day, C.C.s that's all that matters."

Shame burns in my face, hotter than any Arizona summer day.

Jeremy

Jeremy closed his eyes as he reached under Annabelle to grab her teat. He rested his head against her side breathing in her rich earthy smell. Hard ribs pressed back. She was getting thin.

Soon the rhythmic sound of milk hitting the pail filled the darkness. The barn cats appeared for their morning treat. Jeremy rocked back and forth on the stool, occasionally squirting a stream at the cats rubbing at Annabel's hooves. They licked their whiskers and paws, and he laughed.

Thunder rumbled in the distance. He looked up. Strange. There wasn't a cloud in the sky. The low growl stretched out over several seconds, growing in pitch. Jeremy stopped milking and sat back.

Annabelle turned to look at him as he stood. She watched him hurry toward the barn door. Birds swirled overhead, circled the cornfield, and dashed off toward the river.

The early morning sky was brilliant blue. Confounded Jeremy listened as the distant thunder separated into distinct reports, like a pounding of a giant drum.

Those ain't no drums. It's guns. Big ones.

Jeremy rushed back into the barn. Annabelle shifted.

"Sorry, Annabelle, I gotta take a look."

Jeremy scurried up the ladder to the hay loft. The hoist door had a clear view to the southwest. The pounding sounded like it was coming from Ox Road.

Strands of loose hay scattered the loft floor. There had been little enough at the end of the winter. Even less when Union troops moved through and commandeered whatever was left over. Dust motes and flies floated in and out of the sunlight, accompanied by the smell of rotting straw. Jere-my climbed over the lip of the loft. Rays of early morning sun poured through the square hoist opening in the wall. It cast a strip of yellow on the bare boards. The rest of the space was shrouded in shadow.

Jeremy leaned against the door frame and strained his ears. The thunder's rumble stretched into long rolls of continuous booming. A grey cloud rose in the distance and spread out over the trees far to the south.

So, it had begun.

They were so close. A flash of excitement ripped through Jeremy's chest and a cheer burst into his throat.

"Whup them secessionist good-for-nothings. Whup them good."

10

CHARLOTTE

AFTER WE GOT FAR ENOUGH FROM SCHOOL TO BE SURE no one was chasing us, the others finished an entire carton of gummy worms. From there things went downhill fast. Tyler and Scott were crowding me out, anyway. Alexis and Ella certainly didn't seem to notice, so I made some excuse about Mom wanting me home for lunch with her sister, and I ditched the game.

At school Monday, I steer clear of Alexis and Ella. Things had been uncomfortable enough between us but when Tyler and Scott show up, all I want is to pull a disappearing act like the ghost boy.

During our morning break, I find a table at the back of the library and start on my English assignment: *Of Mice and Men.* Between the Battlefield Boy and a candy heist, somehow, I forget to read the first chapter.

I'm trying to focus but have no idea what I'm reading, and I jump about a foot when someone walks up behind me. I gasp and look up directly into Josh Gerber's eyes. They're green it turns out.

"Hey, how's it going?" he says. I find it very hard to speak with my heart pounding in my ears, so I simply nod.

"Now that's what I'm talking about," Isabel says, stepping out from behind him. "You see what a stellar example of scholar-athlete my buddy is, Josh?" She smiles down at me. "She could be outside gossiping, instead, she's working." Apparently, neither of them can hear the beast galloping through my chest.

Isabel sits down and unpacks her books. She shoos Josh off to find a table of his own. "This table is for people with work to do," Isabel says. "We don't have time for your games." Josh fakes a look of shock.

"Fine," he says. "I was thinking about sleeping, anyway. The Nats' game went into extra innings, last night. On the west coast."

I don't read another word of *Of Mice and Men*. Josh makes me jumpy. After a couple of minutes of flipping through a thick textbook in front of her, Isabel sighs.

"So," she says. "How do you like being on the team?"

I shrug. "It's fun," I lie, trying my best to sound upbeat.

"Yeah? Well, good. We certainly can use some girls with speed. Two of our fastest runners graduated last year." I nod and smile.

Then out of nowhere, Isabel asks, "Where'd you go during the game Saturday? I saw you heading toward the concessions and then you disappeared before I could say hi."

Uh oh! Did she see us go in the gym? I struggle to think of an excuse. "We, umm, left early." It's easier to stick with the original lie. "My mom wanted me home. We went to lunch with my aunt."

"Hmmm," she says. "I thought I saw you with Tyler Mays…" She pauses as if she has to think about what to say next. "I just gotta warn you. I've known Tyler since kindergarten. He's trouble. I'd stay away from him if I were you."

I dig my fingernail into some initials carved in the table.

"I think he has a thing for a girl I know. He's not a friend or anything." She's right. He is trouble.

Isabel must notice that I'm uncomfortable because, instead of asking more questions, she tears a piece of paper out of her notebook and changes the subject.

"Need any help with your homework?" she asks. "That is what a team buddy is supposed to do, after all."

I shake my head and reread the same sentence I've been reading for the last ten minutes. "No, I'm good. Thanks," I say.

By the time the bell rings for the next period, I've read a total of one page. So much for catching up with my work during break.

Jeremy

Jeremy squinted down the lane. The afternoon sun had dried up the morning's rain and now, Nate Strumble was kicking up a lot of dust as he ran toward the house. Blue galloped across the field to meet him.

"Mrs. Turner, Mrs. Turner." Most of the time, that boy had a fishing line in the eddies above the falls. What could possibly have gotten him to running?

Jeremy took off his hat and wiped his face against the shoulder of his shirt. He laid down his hoe and stepped between the rows of young corn plants. The boy looked frantic. Blue barked at Nate's heels.

Ma stepped out of the cabin, wiping her hands on her apron. She hushed Blue who bounded up the cabin steps. He sat immediately at Ma's side.

"...cloth and sheets. Momma said it don't matter what, just as long as it's clean." Jeremy caught a few words of what Nate said as he approached the cabin. "They're pouring into town on account of the battle at Manassas Junction. I ain't never seen anything like it. They're bleeding all over the yard."

Ma looked at Jeremy as he came up behind Nate. Her eyes seemed to have caught the fear in the boy's voice.

"Jeremy, hitch up Ginny. We're going into town." She smoothed her apron over her watermelon belly. "I thank thee for the message, Nate. Get going and warn the other women."

Jeremy watched Nate race across the back pasture, kicking up stones. Blue leaping beside him.

"Blue," Jeremy called.

"What are you standing there for, Jeremy. I told you to hitch up Ginny."

"Did Nate say what side the wounded were from?"

Ma stared at him a hard moment. "Does it matter? When thou are dying, it doesn't matter who helps keep death at bay."

Ma turned toward the sound of rumbling in the distance. Jeremy followed her eyes.

"I pray to God that if thy father or uncles are in that nightmare, no one stops to ask his loyalties before they stop his bleeding." Ma's voice shook.

Jeremy squinted at her through one eye.

Rebels started this mess. He turned toward the barn. He'd help because Ma asked him to. But whether a Rebel lived or died meant nothing to him. What he wanted was a chance to shoot some himself.

11

CHARLOTTE

ALEXIS AND ELLA ARE IN RARE FORM THIS WEEK AT lunch. Every chance they have, they sit with Scott Osborne and his friends. Tyler is an 8th grader, so he's nowhere to be seen. The 8th grade lunch is two periods later. While I keep expecting to get called into the principal's office, they act as if nothing at all happened. I might be paranoid, but I'm new to the whole breaking and entering thing.

Today, though Scott isn't sitting with them. They wave me over when they see me looking for a seat.

I stir the rice in the Stonewall Jackson cafeteria's version of Taco Tuesday and do my best to keep up. Apparently, Amanda Frazer and Jack Fine were spending a lot of time together. I have no idea who either of them is, but good for them.

When there's a sudden silence, I glance up at Alexis and Ella. They have their heads together, whispering. They keep glancing at the table a couple of rows over. I follow their eyes and the taco in my stomach almost comes back up. I look away. Josh, Isabel, and some other 8th graders are sitting there eating lunch. Ella and Alexis look at me and smile.

"Charlotte," Ella sings, "You should sit at that table. Isn't that Josh Gerber over there?"

My heart feels like I just finished doing stadiums. And my face is probably just as red.

"Shut up, you guys." Suddenly it's way too hot in the cafeteria.

Tucking my hair behind my ear, I steal a look at the 8th graders. In that instant, Josh looks right at me. He smiles and then elbows Isabel, who sits next to him. He jabs a thumb at our table. She turns, smiles, and waves. Now, I'm not breathing either.

I straighten up and wave back. I do my best to pretend we hadn't just been talking about them. Alexis and Ella watch me and the whole room feels too small, too noisy, and too crowded. I push the "Taco Special," which oozes grease, to the other side of my tray. I'm not hungry anymore. Alexis and Ella giggle, and I can tell they're working up to start in on teasing me. My leg bounces under the table as I scan the room for an escape route. Josh and Isabel stand, pick up their trays, and start toward our table.

"Hey, C.C.," Josh says. Isabel nods a hello.

"Hey" is my response, I think.

"Sorry to burst in on 7th grade lunch. We have an athletic council meeting during our lunch. Fall teams run booths at the Autumn Festival, except football, of course." She rolls her eyes.

"We were just talking about which booth the Cross-Country team should run." Josh says looking at me. "Got a suggestion?"

"I'll think about it," I say, trying to sound helpful. My knee bounces faster.

"Great. We'll be talking about it at practice today," Isabel says. Her voice is light and easy. I'm in full shrinking mode. I can't look at Josh.

"See you at practice," Isabel says as she spins to carry her tray across the cafeteria to the conveyor belt that takes dirty dishes into the kitchen. After a moment, I glance up. Josh turns around, smiles at me, then disappears into a crowd of kids.

Ella and Alexis burst out together in the loudest whisper I've ever heard. "C.C.?!" Now it feels like I've eaten hot chilis.

"He's even got a pet name for you." Alexis says. "That's so cute!" Ella squeals.

"You guys," I look back the way Josh and Isabel went. "He'll hear you."

Alexis and Ella exchange a quick look and then Alexis looks the other way. "Whatever," she says with a shrug.

I look down at my tray.

"You know," Ella says, "Maybe it's time for you to, you know… branch out. Make some more friends. You clearly didn't enjoy hanging with us at the game last weekend."

It feels like I've been punched in the stomach. They're trying to get rid of me.

My eyes throb as the tears build, but I have to keep it together. I need to leave. Now.

I mumble something about having to do math homework, climb out of the bench, and run.

Even though I'm focused on my feet, I feel every eye in the

cafeteria drilling into my back. I push through a swell of kids waiting to scrape their food into the trash, dump my uneaten taco into the bin, and the fork and knife hit the soaking bin with a muffled crash.

With my head down I half run, half stumble toward the cafeteria exit. Before my hands hit the bar to open the door, it flies open. Someone catches me as I crash into the hallway. It's Eric Finson, the boy with the long eyelashes and deep brown eyes from the first day of school.

"Whoa, Dude, slow down," he says as I spin away from him. "Hey, are you okay?"

Double steel doors at the far end of the hall swing easily under my weight. Rows of steel tables line a room I've never been in before. A worker in a white coat and a clear plastic hair net opens a door with a soft click and the whoosh of a seal breaking. The faint smell of refrigeration follows. The hanger in Dover smelled like this: things kept on ice. Dover is where the families of soldiers killed in action go to receive their remains.

"You're not allowed in here." The cafeteria worker glares at me. I cover my face with my hands and retrace my steps, as the memory, of my father lying in a coffin in full dress uniform, chases me down the hallway lined with lockers. Kids stand in clumps, waiting for the bell to signal the beginning of the next class. The clang and crash of locker doors echoes off the tile floor.

I had been in math class, trying to remember the trick for multiplying fractions. The door of the classroom opened and

Mr. Lewis, the principal of my grade school, peeked in and motioned to Ms. Jackson. She didn't even stop talking as she walked toward him. The two whispered then looked straight at me, and I knew.

The principal led me down a hallway just like this one, lined with lockers. He didn't say anything, except that my mother was waiting for me in his office. She didn't have to say anything. The whole story was written on her face. The words hit like a tsunami. "Oh, Honey. It's Daddy."

The fact that my father might never come home from a deployment lay coiled in my heart my whole life. And now it struck like a fanged serpent.

Three weeks before my graduation from 6th grade, my father's personnel carrier ran over an IED in Afghanistan. They say he never felt a thing. It was over too fast, but I can't help going over and over his last seconds. Did he know what was happening? Did he think about me?

Did he know how much I love him?

The second bell rings. My math teacher steps into the hall to close the door. He moves aside to let me in. As the door closes behind me, I know I've only outrun the memory. Like the Battlefield boy, it will be back.

JEREMY

Jeremy turned the wagon onto the road into town. Ahead, the ground itself seemed to churn with movement. Jeremy's stomach tightened at the sight of the seething throng of bleeding men staggering east.

Ma stared straight ahead as they passed a stumbling pair of Yankees whose heads were wrapped in bloody cloths.

"Keep going, Jeremy, these men have bandages, somebody has already tended to them," she said.

Soon, the smell of blood mixed with mud, and the road was teaming with men with red saturated bandages. Boots grate on gravel. From the looks of the wounded, the Rebels had put up quite a fight.

Ginny's head jerked up as someone grabbed her harness.

"Stop, please, help. We need help." The soldier yanked on Ginny's head trying to force the wagon to the side of the road.

A wave of anger surged through Jeremy. "Get off my horse," he shouted.

The wagon lurched as Ginny jerked away from the man in the road. Ma clutched the seat. "We need to get to the front of this chaos," she said.

Moans and curses mixed with threats as Jeremy urged Ginny forward. The flow of wounded men grew thicker until it felt like they were fighting their way up-river. Ginny tossed her head as if to tell him she was doing her best.

The closer to town they got, the more choked with people, carts, horses, and mules the road became, until finally there was no place for Jeremy to steer the wagon. Men moaned from litters begging for a ride, their faces streaked in black soot, like the freakish inverse of ghouls. Others straggled past the wagon. Everywhere Jeremy looked, lips and teeth were stained black from tearing open powder packets to load their guns. The strong dragged the weak. Hair stuck to brows, and sweat-stained shirts hung open, covered in black and streaked with brown. Wounds shone black with blood. Some used crutches fashioned from tree branches. Others groaned from wagon beds, or across horse backs, or on blankets by the side of the road. The smell of human excrement was everywhere. The street looked slick and treacherous.

"Let me out here," Ma ordered when he couldn't move Ginny another inch. "Help me unload the cart." She looked around unsure where to step down.

"Get some of the worst of these men into the wagon and double back," she said. Take the northern road into town. The road ahead looks too clogged for us to get through to the Strumble place. Lord knows she'll have to manage by herself. We have our share of work to do here."

Jeremy tied Ginny's reins to the buckboard's rail. He leapt into the crowd. The stench of sweat mixed with gunpowder, urine, and worse overpowered him. It was the smell of defeat. Jeremy looked around at the sea of blue uniforms. These were Union soldiers. He knew just looking at them, the South had won the battle.

How could the Rebels beat the US Army?

Jeremy stumbled at the press of men and reached in over the wagon's rail. Ma held a pile of cloth, red streaked her sleeve and trailed down her skirt. Blue sat patiently in the flatbed of the truck, staring out above the chaos, like he didn't want to see.

Someone grabbed Jeremy's leg. The grip seemed to cut into his skin. He looked down into the face of a young boy, not much older than he was.

"Help me," the boy said. His eyes seemed disconnected from his voice. "I want to go home." His voice quavered. "Please, tell my momma. Have mercy, please?"

Jeremy looked at Ma, who struggled toward them. She stooped down and loosened the boys grip on Jeremy. Blood now smeared Jeremy's grey pants.

"I'll help you, soldier. Just lie quietly while I cut bandages." Ma put her hand behind the boy's head as she eased him into a lying position exposing a tattered black hole in his side. It oozed white and black liquid. Ma looked up at Jeremy.

"Rip a portion of that bedding. Quickly." Strain shook her voice and hands. "It's a wonder he made it this far." Jeremy tore a section of the sheets. When he turned back to Ma, she was whispering to herself as she closed the boy's eyes.

"He'll not suffer anymore," she said. "His mother's agony will haunt her always, I'm afraid." She turned toward the seething crowd of other wounded men. "Now we must attend the living."

12

CHARLOTTE

ALEXIS AND ELLA DIDN'T EVEN GLANCE AT ME THE whole class, so I lug my backpack to the library after math. I find a carrel at the back and pull my father's laptop out of my backpack. I need to start on my response to the English reading. If I get through the rest of the afternoon without losing it again, maybe we can pretend nothing at all happened at lunch.

Not likely, I know.

Then I open my laptop and find the last page I looked at, a YouTube video about a boy on Manassas Battlefield, who disappeared after talking to a guy with a black Labrador. Just like Beau.

Soon, I'm deep into a new hunt. Maybe this Ranger Vanderly guy knows something.

My search for Ranger Vanderly shows that he used to be on staff at the park but recently retired. There's no contact info, but he is on Facebook. I click the link, even though I don't have an account.

Damn. "FORBIDDEN" screams at me from a red and black textbox.

"Well, well, well. Caught red-handed."

Josh?!

"I'm …uh, I had to…it's for history research." Forget it, Charlotte Cross, you're busted.

"Facebook for history research. This I have to hear."

"No, I ...need... to find someone."

You sound like an idiot. Just close your mouth.

I can't look at him.

He sits down in the seat beside me smelling of wood smoke and leather. If he tells Isabel he caught me doing anything but studying, she'll get all serious on me again.

"Please don't tell Isabel." The hairs on my neck tingle. "I'm just…"

"I can see you were 'just.'"

"Mr. Gerber, I assume you are discussing schoolwork over there." Mr. Hodges, the school librarian stands at the end of the row of books staring at us.

"You bet, Mr. Hodges." Josh looks at me and shrugs. "I'd close that window if I were you," he whispers. "You know how Mr. Hodges is about social media."

There's that smile again.

Isabel walks up at that very moment. She tosses her backpack onto the carrel on my other side.

"Well, people," she says, "you can thank me later for getting us out of Moon Bounce duty. We got doughnuts."

"Good job!" Josh says and they bump fists.

Isabel looks at me. "Last year's Homecoming was a disaster. Some kid threw up in that thing, and we spent hours cleaning it out."

Josh nods and makes a disgusted face. "Nightmare is more like it. I get nauseous just thinking about it."

"Mr. Gerber, Ms. Price. This is your last warning." Mr. Hodges sounds angry. Josh looks at Isabel and then over her shoulder. I peek around the corner of the carrel. "Back to work," he whispers and then throws a fake punch at Isabel that she dodges easily.

Mr. Hodges starts down the aisle in our direction. "You three are going to have to break it up."

"Sure, Mr. Hodges," Josh says. He doesn't look back at me. Thank God.

Of course, I get nothing done. When the end of class bell rings, I shove my ancient computer back in my backpack. As the three of us walk toward the library exit, I do my best to act normal, whatever that means. At the hallway we turn in opposite directions.

"See you at practice," Isabel says, as I glance back at them and nod.

"Yep," I say. "See ya."

Jeremy

July 28, 1861

Jeremy stood by Ginny's head, fiddling with the harness outside Mr. Lyons store, while Blue sniffed at a pile of horse manure in the street. For the first time since Virginia seceded and Pa left, Jeremy and Ma rode beyond the Rebel pickets to get provisions in Manassas.

Leveled trees lining the roads, and the charred remains of wagons and artillery pieces, proved what Jeremy already knew. The Union had gotten a thrashing. What was worse, the entire county seemed to be in town celebrating. Everybody except Ma and Jeremy.

Folks were smiling and greeting one another like Christmas had come early. Jeremy wondered if anyone knew Pa had skedaddled North.

They had heard nothing from him. Shame and anger gnawed at Jeremy as he watched the women gather on the street across from Lyon's store. They hugged and laughed like they'd won the war already.

Ma insisted on coming into town to check for mail and get the supplies they needed. The summer heat had shriveled the vegetables and Union troops managed to trample everything else as they fled the battle. Didn't matter what Uncle

Charles said, the Union could barely defend itself. No one was looking out for them.

Except him.

"After I finish at Mr. Lyon's, I must talk to Mrs. Whitehead, Jeremy. I may be a while." Mrs. Whitehead would be the mid-wife. No denying it, then. Ma was having a baby. Pa didn't even know.

At the end of the road, a band began a funeral march. Ginny glanced up, and Ma and Jeremy watched a wagon, loaded with a coffin, move at a snail's pace in their direction.

"The price of victory, I'm afraid." A man stood in front of a rocker on the store's porch.

He removed his hat as the wagon passed. "That's the third one today."

An older man and several women in black, one holding the hands of two small children, shuffled past, the women lifting veils and dabbing at their eyes. A boy, clutching a musket that looked twice his size, glared at the crowd.

No one spoke as the funeral passed.

Ma turned and trudged up the store's stairs holding her skirts. She disappeared into the building.

Jeremy unhitched Ginny from the wagon, led her a few times around in the shade and then to the water trough. Blue sat scratching under the building's steps. Several men leaned against the store's back wall. One lounged in a rocker fanning himself with his wide-brimmed straw hat, watching a line of men that trailed past the building.

"With such a fine-looking array of manhood, the South can't loose," the man said to no one in particular. The others murmured their agreement.

The men in line in the road shifted in the sun. Some rested the butts of their muskets on the ground beside them. Others clutched thick leather cases or fanned themselves with folded papers. Jeremy watched the line inch its way down the street, through the alley between the store and the next building, and down the street behind the store. What could be so important that so many darn fools would stand in a line in the blazing heat like that? He tied Ginny to the store's rail, then hurried down the road. Blue trotted close behind.

A man in uniform sat at a small desk in the middle of the alley at the front of the line, examining papers of the man in front of him. Beside him another soldier peered into a man's eyes. Other soldiers lounged in the shade.

Recruiters. He should have known. Jeremy watched for a moment then headed toward the front of the store.

A horse pulling a flatbed cart stopped as he reached the stairs. The driver climbed across the seat into the back and tossed a bundle of newspapers onto the porch. The men sitting on the porch lunged for the pile. They shoved each other trying to get their hands on a paper reminding Jeremy of watching the Dawson family scrambling for dinner.

Mr. Lyons burst through the door of the store. "Alright, gentleman, no need to wrestle. Here's one for you all to share."

The cart and horse trotted off. Jeremy watched. Men leaned over the shoulder of the man scanning the front page.

"Well, for the love of God, Tom, would you let a man breathe?" He shrugged the man behind him off.

"You heard old man Lyons. Read the blame thing so all of us can hear." Several men on the porch nodded.

"All right, all right," the first man cleared his throat.

"Victory at Manassas." His voice sounded like he was sitting in the bottom of a barrel. "The Army of General Johnston met the Army of General Scott in the first great battle of this conflict on July 21, and the Confederate States of America emerged victorious!'" Jeremy was surrounded by Rebels, and they were celebrating their victory.

The man's voice grew louder with each sentence. "The soldiers of the Confederacy answered the call to defend their proud and mighty country demonstrating bravery, loyalty, and determination in the face of a foe who was both better equipped and superior in number."

Jeremy hid in the shadow. From the sound of the guns he heard and the wounded men he saw, it had been a cruel day for both sides.

"The battle raged from the first light of that unholy Sunday until well into the late afternoon. When the dust and smoke of the fury receded, the Confederate flag waved victorious over that bloodied field."

The crowd listening began to swell. Jeremy felt sick. As the others strained to hear over the voices around him, he couldn't get the sight, sounds, and smells of the wounded and dead out of his mind.

He willed himself to close out the man's voice, praying and hoping with all his might that Pa had been far away from that hell.

13

CHARLOTTE

WHEN I FINALLY HEAD OUT TO THE INFIELD TO STRETCH, Josh and Isabel are leaving the track for the road.

It has been such a roller coaster ride of a day, all I can do is put my head down, force my muscles, lungs, and legs to take over and run. The rhythm of my feet on the road, the sound of my breathing, the pounding of my heart distract me until I round the last curve of the battlefield. I look for the Battlefield Boy, for *Jeremy*. An ache spreads in my chest.

He's not there.

Circling the giant bronze statue of Stonewall Jackson, I run like I'm being chased. But there he is leaning against the plinth like he's waiting for me. Our eyes meet, and he stands up. He watches me run toward him. Should I stop? Does anyone else see him? I look away and surge down the hill toward school.

It feels like I just turned my back on a friend. But I truly have no idea what I'm supposed to do.

He's a freaking ghost!

The last mile and a half back to school I fly. As I cross the finish line on the school's track for the final 400 meters of the route, Coach Elsberry presses his stopwatch and checks his clip board.

"Good, time, Charlotte," he calls. "Stretch and hit the showers."

I nod and gulp air. Twenty minutes later, I heave my backpack onto my shoulder and lean into the school's glass front doors. The sky is an impossible shade of blue. Kids from all different teams are hanging out on the massive boulders on the school's front lawn. Josh's lean frame jumps into focus. Somehow, I find him in the crowd, no matter who else is there or what else is happening. Forget butterflies. There's a whole flock of geese in my stomach.

Josh and Isabel are standing in a circle with a bunch of other 8th graders I haven't met.

Isabel looks at me, elbows Josh in the side, then says, "Here she comes now. Why don't you ask her yourself?"

Everybody turns to look. I try to stay calm. The flock of geese that was battering my insides, is now circling frantically. Josh looks over his shoulder at me. I look at Isabel. "You wanted to ask me something?"

Josh smiles and my insides go from swirled to churning.

"We were just talking about your time today. You set a new girls' record for the Battlefield loop. Coach looked like he'd won the lottery."

"Wow!" one of the girls listening says, "We could use some strong runners in soccer. It's a spring sport. You should try out."

"Hey you all, back off," Isabel said. "It isn't even September. She's running with us at the moment." The others laugh and their attention shifts to something else. Josh is still smiling at me though. Now a psycho drummer seems to have taken up residence in my chest. I look at the ground, but I can't help it. My eyes find his.

"You ran the Battlefield loop in under 20 minutes. The last time one of our girls did that was 2014," Josh says. "That was Theresa Little. She did it in 19:56. You beat her time by 3 seconds. That's pretty fast, Charlotte Cross," Josh says.

"Hmm." I didn't know what else to say.

"I just thought you'd like to know." Josh's eyes are focused on me. I don't look up, but from the heat in my face, it's definitely turning bright red.

The silence lingers another couple of seconds. "I got to go," I say and back away. Four steps down the driveway, Josh appears at my side.

"Where're you hurrying off to?" He nudges me gently with his elbow. My entire body reacts like I've been shocked.

"I got to get home, that's all." *There, that sounds almost normal.*

"I'll walk you part of the way; I think you live in my direction?"

Do I?

"Coach was really excited," he says after a few moments. "Some of our guys have never run that fast even on their best days."

"Hmm." So, he wants to talk about running.

We walk a few steps in silence. He's so close I can smell

him – wood smoke and soap. "So, I noticed you were at the football game, last weekend. Do you like football?"

"I guess. My dad played when he was in school," I say. "He played for the high school here, actually."

"Cool," Josh says sounding distracted. "Well, a bunch of us go just to hang out. You should come with us."

Before I can answer a strong wind rolls down the pike out of nowhere. It's the kind of wind that usually says a huge thunderstorm is brewing, but there isn't even a hint of clouds in the sky. Then I smell it, fireworks. I look up and stop dead. My knees shake.

"No!" My scalp prickles. Jeremy is standing twenty feet down the sidewalk in front of me. How did he find me here?

Josh walks a few steps forward, then turns around to look at me. His smile disappears. "Are you okay?"

I lower my head. Willing my voice not to give out, I ask, "Do you see that guy in suspenders up the street?"

He looks up. "No," he answers. Then, "Charlotte?" Josh is calling my name, but it sounds like it's coming from far away.

I am not imagining this. The Battlefield Boy, Jeremy is standing there. So why can't Josh see him?

In the next second, Josh grabs my hand, and pulls me across the street. Horns blare.

He leads me to a booth at the McDonald's. The next thing I know, I'm sitting at the back of the restaurant, away from the door and the counter.

Thoughts circle my brain like a dog chasing its tail. When Josh slides into the booth opposite me, he pushes a tall Mc-

Donald's cup toward me. Beads of moisture cling to its surface. What am I going to do?

"I'm not crazy," I say.

"Well, I'm glad we cleared that up," Josh says, stirring his milkshake. "But here's the problem. People who are crazy al-ways say they aren't. So why don't you just tell me what's going on since I'm the one who will have to tell the coach that the secret weapon he thinks he found won't be able to run after all be-cause 'she's crazy,'" he says using air quotes.

"Where do I start?"

"Well start with this guy you just asked me about and go from there."

So, the story spills out of me from the first battlefield run, to the YouTube video, to what happened to Dad.

He doesn't say a thing and his eyes never leave mine while he listens to the whole strange tale.

"He's a ghost," I say finally. "And I have to help him some-how." I don't say it, but maybe if I help him, some-one along a road in Afghanistan, will help my father, too.

Josh sits quietly, sipping his soda. The fact that he doesn't stand up and walk away makes me stronger. We stir our drinks.

"So how are you supposed to help him?

He believes me. A wave of relief makes me lightheaded.

"Who knows." I take a long sip from my drink. It's choc-olate. Of course, he knew to get me chocolate.

"Please don't tell Coach Elsberry I'm nuts." I glance out

the window behind him. The streetlights outside are beginning to glow orange. I look at my watch.

6:00!

"Oh, my God! My mother is going to kill me!"

Before he can say a word, I'm sprinting down the sidewalk toward home.

Jeremy

Ma clutched the buckboard seat, with her lips pressed tight shut. Their heads swayed in time as the wagon rocked side to side.

The wheels of the cart rumbled, and Ginny's hooves clopped hollowly on the planks of the low wooden bridge over Fox Creek. Grey clouds pressed down on them and rumbling of thunder rolled over the trees. A storm had snuck up on them. They were going to get caught in it. Ma sat straight backed with her eyes closed.

Ginny slouched forward dragging the weight of the wagon, her head nodding with each step. She was getting too old to pull the wagon up these muddy hills. She would never have survived the army.

Jeremy handed Ma the reins and hopped off the side of the wagon. He hurried up beside Ginny, grabbed the rein close to Ginny's bit with one hand and the cart's shaft with the other and added his weight to the effort to move the wagon up the hill.

"Come on, Girl. We'll stop up ahead." Ginny's ears flicked once at the sound of his voice. The harness and blinders kept her from turning her head, but she seemed to dig in harder as they climbed the hill.

Jeremy pushed. The wood bit at his palms and fingers. His arms ached, and his breathing quickened.

Poor Ginny. The wagon was heavy.

At the crest of the hill Jeremy caught Ginny's reins and coaxed her to a standstill under a tree. She sighed. Jeremy patted her neck and mopped his face with the sleeve of his shirt. Ma stood, balancing herself on the rocking cart. " We'll give her a rest," she said.

Jeremy pressed two fingers under the girth around Ginny's belly. They came out sticky with her sweat. As he stood up, he caught a glimpse of movement in the woods across the road. The crunch of leaves attracted Blue's attention, too. The dog stood up and stared into the woods. Two Union soldiers, with guns pointed at Jeremy and Ma stepped onto the road. Heat rushed up Jeremy's back and flashed in his face. Ma stiffened.

A third soldier, with his gun raised to his shoulder stepped out of the woods directly behind Jeremy. He was caught like a fox trapped by the hounds.

"Ma'am, please step down from the wagon." The officer in front spoke to Ma as he eyed Jeremy.

"Well, good afternoon, officer. I was just getting to that. Unfortunately, I don't move as fast as I should these days." Jeremy started around Ginny to help Ma.

"Wait right there, Son," The third soldier stepped forward and pushed his gun into the back of Jeremy's head. Jeremy stopped and spread his arms up in front of him, palms open. He'd never had a gun pointed at him like this before. His heart galloped and sweat prickled his scalp. The eyes of one of the other two soldiers twitched. Jeremy held his breath.

The second soldier closest to Ma hurried forward and held out a hand to help her down from the wagon. She took it as she watched the third. Blue's hackles rose.

"Hush, Blue. Come." Blue leaped down from the wagon's bed and sat by Ma's feet.

Ginny shook her harness.

"Please move over here where we can see you, Son. No one need get hurt."

"Surely you've made some mistake, Officer," Ma said. "We've just been to town to replenish our supplies."

"Ma'am, our orders are to stop all traffic coming from that quadrant. No one gets through without express written permission from our commander." A crow swooped low over the wagon and landed on the side of the road; its black wings seemed luminescent in the fading light. "If you don't have a pass, you can't go any further down this road."

"Gentleman, my name is Mrs. John Turner. My son, Jeremy and I live a mile off Georgetown Pike, near the falls. How do you propose that we get a pass if we didn't need one to go into town?"

"Ma'am, I have no intention of letting you pass unless you can prove to me you aren't a Rebel spy."

Ma straightened her shoulders. "I see." She looked at Jeremy. "I don't know your name, Lieutenant, but please have your man lower that gun away from my son's head. Then I will gladly answer your questions. You can see plainly my son is not armed." The soldier nodded and the pressure at the back of Jeremy's head released. He seethed at himself. His hunting gun was tucked behind the buckboard's seat.

Why hadn't he had it with him?

"Now," Ma continued, "if you send one of your party into Alexandria in search of Colonel Charles Turner and ask him to verify the residence of his sister-in-law, Mrs. John Turner, I'm sure he will satisfy your commanding officer." Ma sounded calm. Jeremy recognized the tone, though. Anger brewed beneath the surface.

"You want me to believe that Colonel Turner has kin in these parts? If you are his sister-in-law, why aren't you back home in Philadelphia where good loyal citizens belong?" The gun pressed back into Jeremy's head.

"I don't see the relevance of that question."

The officer probably didn't expect her to have so much fight in her.

"As I said before, I don't know your name, but I know my brother-in-law would greatly appreciate hearing about the assistance you gave his sister-in-law and nephew. Or has disrespecting the lives and bodies of loyal United States citizens become the standard practice within President Lincoln's army?"

Jeremy noticed a bead of sweat rising on her lip. Her hand on Blue's head trembled. "Of course, he might be just as interested to hear of our difficulties." The two men in front of Jeremy conferred in whispers. Ma looked at Jeremy. Her eyes softened for a moment, then she raised her chin and looked back as the two men whispered. Her expression now was more ornery than anything.

"Mrs. Turner, my Sergeant here is inclined to believe you are who you say you are and has volunteered to ride to Colonel Turner's headquarters to verify your story. He is willing to take the consequences if he is wrong.

"You understand of course, that if your tale proves false, you will be arrested." Ma didn't flinch.

Dang fool. He doesn't know who he's up against.

"If you are who you say you are, we will return with the appropriate papers for you. We will allow you to pass after we search your wagon."

"I certainly will not submit to such an affront to my loyal-ty. You know my brother-in-law's reputation. We are members of the Society of Friends. My son has pledged to refrain from violence and will not take up arms. Neither of us supports Vir-ginia's rebellion. That will have to be good enough for you." Jer-emy's heart stung. Now she was making him out to be a coward. He was no Quaker.

The two Yankees conferred again. Finally, the lieutenant set his shoulders and sneered. "You better be who you say you are or neither of you will last an hour in Point Lookout." The officer spat the mention of the federal prison out like a cuss word.

As Jeremy climbed back into the wagon, he heard Blue growl at the man with his gun trained on Jeremy's head.

Ma never flinched.

14

CHARLOTTE

I NEXT SEE JOSH WANDERING AROUND OUTSIDE THE GATE at the football game Saturday morning. He's got his hands in his pockets, like he's waiting for someone.

Even though it's still hot and technically summer, there's something about football that's tied up with fall and watching football games with Dad. When he was home, Dad and I watched every Virginia Tech game together.

Alexis and Ella show up finally. I'm relieved they don't walk in the other direction when they see me. They're the only friends I have in 7th grade. Maybe it's because they spot Josh a second or two after I do and immediately, Ella elbows me in the ribs.

"Look who's here," she says a trill in her voice. I nod, not sure what to say to him.

Alexis and Ella don't know about the shake he bought me. I won't tell them the other stuff. They've already written me off as a loser. Not to mention the fact that I still can't believe the Battlefield Boy is a ghost.

When Josh sees us, he smiles and drifts over. Ella and Alexis wear huge smiles. "Hi, Josh," they say in unison, like they've practiced it or something. He nods at them and then asks, "Hey, have you seen Isabel? We were supposed to meet up with a couple 8th graders."

So not me he's looking for.

His face lights up. "There they are," he says, and he charges off toward the stands. As he trots off, he turns around and calls, "See ya!"

My heart stings with the disappointment. He didn't invite me to go with him. But Ella's and Alexis's faces make me flinch. They're looking at me like there's something gross smeared all over my face.

"Nice," Ella says, but her tone says the opposite. "Good move, Charlotte. You gotta do better than that." That's the last thing they say before the band starts up and drowns out any possibility of a conversation. I follow them, even though I clearly am not wanted. What else can I do? I don't really know anyone else here, and Josh has disappeared. Ella and Alexis climb the bleachers to the very top row. Scott and Tyler show up about halfway through the second quarter. They claim seats a row in front of us and soon I'm the only one watching the game. For a middle school team, the Stonewall Varsity is pretty good. Well, at least they seem to have more than one play, anyway. Dad would have liked coming to the games. Missing him stings so much.

When the half-time whistle blows, Scott, and Tyler stand up. "Hungry?" Ella asks no one in particular.

"I could eat," Alexis answers hopping up, too. Tyler claps his hands and moves toward the stairs. In the next moment, I'm panicking. It took the whole week for my heart to stop leaping out of my chest and landing on the floor every time I saw the principal after last week's game.

No way I'm doing that again.

Ella grins at Alexis and she follows Tyler down the bleacher stairs. "I think I'll pass," I shout in Alexis's ear. Alexis shrugs but before they even reach the bottom step, sitting there, way up at the top of the bleachers all alone, I look like loser. I run to catch up with them. As we wind our way behind the food trailers, Scott is pulling Ella by the arm and walking backwards. You'd think he had some kind of surprise for her, not a raid on the food closet.

The banging of my heart makes it impossible to breathe, let alone think of an excuse to get out of what is about to go down. As the others duck into the gym, I hang back.

I can't do it.

At that moment, Josh waves to me from the hot dog line. He smiles, says something to one of the kids in the group around him and jogs over.

"Hey," he says as if it's completely normal for him to be chatting with me.

"Hey," I say, glancing at the gym door. Thick cables leading to the food trucks prevent it from closing all the way.

"Your friends go?" He's all smiles, as if nothing at all happened the day before, like I hadn't spilled my guts out telling him all about my dad, the move, and a ghost. "You can hang out with us if you want. We're getting food, then sitting as far from the band as possible."

I shrug. Would abandoning Ella and Alexis mean I'm doing better? What did that even mean anyway?

"Ummm, I'm not sure..."

At that moment, Ella sticks her head out the gym door. "There you are. Tyler said you chickened out." She stops when she sees Josh and steps outside. The door bangs against the cables, keeping the door from closing.

"Oh, hi, Josh."

In the next second the door crashes open. Alexis and Scott take off, knocking Ella into me. Ella runs after them. Josh grabs the door to keep it from banging into us. Next, Tyler flies out of the gym, followed immediately by the school security guard who nabs the back of Tyler's shirt.

"Don't move!" he shouts at me as he collars Josh, who's still holding the door open.

I freeze.

Josh looks confused.

"Thought you'd help yourself to some free snacks?" the security guard asks. "Well, I've got news for you. You three are about to be expelled."

Josh swears.

Me? I'm wishing I could pull the Battlefield Boy's trick and disappear.

JEREMY

December 29, 1861

A crinkled voice wormed its way into Jeremy's brain. "Come on, Boy. Wake up."

Jeremy fought opening his eyes and when he did the dim morning light showed the pinched face of Mrs. Whitehead.

What was she still doing here? She'd been talking to Ma when he fell asleep.

A groan rose from Ma's room. Jeremy jumped up and peered through the door. Ma lay in bed, her face glistening in the firelight. Her head rocked back and forth on the pillow. Even Annabelle didn't sound that bad when she needed milking. What was he supposed to do?

Mrs. Whitehead touched his arm. "Don't worry, Boy. Your Momma's time has come. It's just the baby. Thank good fortune I stopped in last night. Not a minute too soon, I'd say."

Jeremy glanced out of the corner of his eye at Ma. Mrs. Whitehead urged him toward the table. A hunk of bread and a fried egg waited for him on a plate. Blue sat at his feet staring at Ma's bedroom door.

Jeremy swallowed the coarse bread, then Mrs. Whitehead handed him his coat and scarf.

"This is no place for a boy. Go on. I'm sure there is some work for you to be doing this morning." She put her hand on the latch of the cabin's door.

A blast of frigid air and pale predawn light streamed in as she stepped out of the way to let him pass. Jeremy looked behind him as he crossed in front of Mrs. Whitehead. Ma moaned. He'd never heard her sound so sick.

Mrs. Whitehead closed the door behind him. A second later, the cabin door opened, and Blue scurried out. The door slammed shut again.

Crisp air tickled Jeremy's nose and he wound the scratchy wool scarf around his neck, then pulled on his patched coat. He held as still as stone and listened.

Outside, Ma's groans sounded muffled. A second later her voice grew louder then she went silent. Jeremy felt his heart plummet to his feet.

Was she dying?

Snow crunched under his feet as he crossed the yard. He yanked open the door of the barn and stepped into the silence.

The warm air and heavy smell of animal dung, old straw, and sweat enfolded him. Two pairs of moist dark eyes stared through the dim light. Annabelle and Ginny seemed to be expecting him. He trudged over to the cow's pen, leaned against the coarse wood and swallowed hard. His eyes stung.

"Ma's having the baby," he said. The cow blinked at him. Blue sat down in the center of the barn. He looked worried, too.

Jeremy watched the door for a moment. Annabelle mooed.

He rubbed his nose with the back of his glove. "I expect I know what you want. No use in putting it off. It only makes the work multiply." Now he sounded like Ma. He retrieved the pail and milking stool and set to work. The cats appeared from somewhere in the shadows. They rubbed against Annabelle's legs. Good old Annabelle sure was patient.

The cow's teat was warm and soft to his fingers. He pressed his face into her coarse fur. Annabelle's familiar scent, mixed with the sweet aroma of milk steaming in the bucket, calmed him some. Ma would be alright. Women had babies all the time. Ma had had other babies. One had even lived for a few weeks.

Something else nagged at him, though. The Sullivan family who sat up in the front pew of church had no momma at all, but seven little ones sat all in a row like dolls next to their daddy. Little fingers of fear crept up Jeremy's spine. Mrs. Sullivan had died having Samuel.

He couldn't think about that. He focused on milking Annabelle, and before he knew it, two pails of milk stood steaming in the corner. He fed both animals, mucked the stalls, and brushed Ginny. Her thick winter coat gave off clouds of dust. Pa would have his hide if he saw how dirty she was. Old straw lay in moldy heaps by the barn door. The air was thick with its smell. Well at least he had managed to lay in some feed for the winter.

Jeremy climbed the ladder to the loft and pushed his fists

deep into the pockets of his coat. His fingers and toes felt like solid blocks of ice, and his wool sweater itched. He slid his back down the wall and tried to distract himself from thoughts of the warm fire in the cabin.

Nothing would happen to Ma. She was strong, not so skinny like Mrs. Sullivan had been.

He laid his face against the tops of his knees and closed his eyes.

Jeremy hated waiting.

15

CHARLOTTE

BY THE TIME MOM ARRIVES AT THE PRINCIPAL'S OFFICE Tyler has been hauled off someplace. He had a joint in his pocket, and, for some reason, he was carrying a switchblade.

I don't know where Josh was taken, but I'm alone, sitting in the chair opposite Mr. Philip's desk while Mom and he have a conversation outside the door.

When the door finally opens, Principal Philips lets Mom in the room.

Mom's look is a cross between, "I'm totally confused" and "You are in so much trouble." She's angry, but not out of her mind mad.

"Your mother and I have talked, Miss Cross. I have impressed upon her that being in the school building on a weekend without permission is a serious violation of the regulations. While we cannot connect you directly to the activities of the three students who were discovered in the gym and the missing items, the security guard got a clear sight of the three he chased. From their descriptions, they are all friends of yours..." He pauses as if he thinks I'm going to tell on them.

He'd asked me a hundred times in fifty different ways to tell him who they were and what they were doing in the gym. The only thing I would say is that Josh didn't do anything.

His crime—being stupid enough to get caught talking to me. I can't imagine what he thinks of me now.

"I've told your mother that under the circumstances, we're not suspending you. But you're on academic probation with an in-school suspension. That means you'll need to report to Assistant Principal Cummings's office for all your free periods, lunches, and recesses for the next two weeks. During that time, you're prohibited from attending any extracurricular activities or to participate in any campus events on the weekends, including Cross Country. You also have two weeks' worth of detention."

No running!

Principal Phillips looks sad, like he's disappointed to have to say all of this.

"If you are caught in the building without permission outside of school hours one more time, I will suspend you for real. A third violation will mean expulsion…" He pauses again. "Do you understand?" he asks, staring at me.

I lower my head and nod.

In the car, Mom doesn't say a word as she drives me home. As we pull up to the house, she wonders out loud, "What do you think your father would say right now?"

The words sting. Dad repeated the military code of honor like a mantra: respect, duty, loyalty, service, integrity, and personal courage.

He would have said I'd let him down.

Jeremy

Blue stood up, waking Jeremy from a light doze. He stuck his face over the edge of the loft. The dog stared at the barn door; his head cocked to one side. In a moment, the door swung open, and Mrs. Whitehead poked her head in.

"Boy?" she called, looking for him. When she spotted him at the top of the ladder, she sounded annoyed. "There you are." Mrs. Whitehead's face seemed even more wrinkled now than it had earlier. "Come on, boy; your momma wants to see you."

Something in his throat made it hard for Jeremy to swallow. He shivered. Blue danced so close to the base of the ladder that Jeremy had to jump from the third rung to avoid stepping on him. His feet throbbed as he hit the ground. Mrs. Whitehead drew her gray shawl tighter around her shoulders as she passed through the door in front of him.

"It's freezing out here," she said.

Light reflecting off the snow stung Jeremy's eyes as Blue bounded ahead, his tail wagging, then he trotted back to Jeremy. Jeremy's mouth went dry.

Blue knows something. What if…? He pushed the thought away and approached the door, hesitating.

Please, Ma, be alright.

The door gave way under Jeremy's weight, but he opened it just a crack. Blue pushed on the door and scooted in under Jeremy's arm.

"Well, go on in." Mrs. Whitehead called. With one hand out to the side and the other clasping her shawl, she gingerly picked her way across the packed snow to the cabin door. "Your momma's waiting."

A crack of light pierced the dark cabin through the drapes drawn tight against the cold. The silhouettes of the table and rocker came into shape in the orange pool of firelight that stretched across the floor from the hearth. Jeremy approached Ma's door.

Blue whirled in circles and bowed in the middle of Ma's room, his entire body beckoning to Jeremy to hurry. Jeremy slipped to the bedside and knelt down as Ma rolled her head on the pillow.

Was she dying? Could she talk?

Ma's hand lay on her chest and rode up and down with the slow rise and fall of her breathing. He lowered his face to the quilt draped over her.

"There thee are, my love." Her hand reached to him and stroked his hair. She looked at Jeremy through puffy eyes. Her hair stuck to her face and neck. Ma blinked, smiled, and laughed. Jeremy's throat tightened. She hadn't laughed in the longest time.

A soft snuffling squeak came from a bu ndle lying next to Ma. A corner of the blanket embroidered with Jeremy's name and birthday moved slightly, revealing an oval patch of pink skin.

"Jeremy, meet Sarah," Ma's voice sounded weak. A squished-up face with an ugly blue tint jerked back and forth. It snuffled again. "She's named for my mother. Isn't she beautiful?"

Jeremy squinted. How could anything so wrinkled and blue be beautiful?

"She's borrowing thy quilt. I hope thee don't mind." The baby yawned a long, exhausted yawn exposing a tiny set of gums. Something unfamiliar stirred in Jeremy's chest.

She was so small.

Ma lifted her hand from Jeremy's hair and moved the blanket away from the pink cheek. Sarah turned her face toward Ma's touch. Her eyelids fluttered, and small slits of gray-blue peaked out at him.

Mrs. Whitehead patted Jeremy's shoulders. He swallowed and wiped his hand across his eyes, then on his trousers.

"Come on now, boy; get out of those frozen things. You've traipsed enough snow through the cabin to keep an entire summer's worth of stores."

Jeremy stood up but lingered near the bed. He didn't want to go just yet.

"Your mother's had a hard time of it. Don't fret, she's strong. Just let her sleep for a while. She'll be back to herself in no time." Mrs. Whitehead stepped away. Jeremy looked down at Ma and the baby lying beside her. Mrs. Whitehead nudged him toward the main room and closed the door to the bedroom. She busied herself with a kettle and pot hanging in the hearth.

"Your aunt will be here in a day or two. I sent her word a week ago that you mother's time was approaching. How she'll get a pass this deep behind the lines, I don't know. I guess even the army respects a woman's needs in childbirth."

Mrs. Whitehead talked, but she didn't seem to expect Jeremy to respond. She rocked gently in the rocking chair, cradling a teacup.

"I've been trying to convince your mother that you all would be better off moving in with her parents until this mess is done and over with, or even, God forbid, to your Pa's family in Philadelphia. Only makes sense to get out of the path of this war. No one ever heeds my advice it seems. Your mother is intent on staying where your father's letters can find you. Ah, well, some people don't know what's good for them, I'm afraid."

Leave the farm?

The black kettle started a slow steamy thrumming and soon silenced Mrs. Whitehead with a screech. She took both the kettle and the soup pot from the long iron arm that stretched into the hearth, poured hot water into her cup of tea, and then filled the bowl for Jeremy with soup.

"Come have your soup now, boy. No use starving. I did the best I could with what was in the larder. Not as much as turnip to gnaw on, mind you. You'd think your mother had been idle all summer. No matter, there's not much anywhere now, anyway."

Mrs. Whitehead sat down in the rocker close to the foot of Jeremy's bed. She closed her eyes and leaned her head back.

Jeremy sipped the hot contents of his bowl. The salty broth cleared the lump that had lodged in his throat. He stared into the long red flames of the fire. Blue circled twice before settling down on the hearth.

Ma looked so weak lying there. Jeremy ignored the nagging dread that had snuck into his heart.

He wouldn't leave the farm, not unless it was to join the fight. No matter what Ma had to say about it.

16

CHARLOTTE

WHEN I GET TO SCHOOL ON MONDAY, THERE'S A NOTE stuffed into the slats of my locker from the school's administration reminding me that I cannot participate in sports as long as I'm on in-school suspension. Coach Elsberry has been informed

"Was it bad?" Alexis asks as I close my locker, shoving the office note into my back pocket. Ella clutches her books close to her chest and looks down the hall. Mom had confiscated my phone, but neither of them had tried to get a hold of me. Not even email to find out what happened. As far as I know, their parents weren't even called. I guess the security guard didn't get that good a look at them after all.

I shrug. "It was mostly quiet," I say. "I can't run until I do two weeks of detention.

"Yeah, we heard," she says.

How had they heard?

"Do you know what happened to Josh?" I ask. Alexis and Ella shake their heads.

"Tyler got suspended. It isn't his first one," Alexis says.

"They're talking about expelling him." Ella says.

We walk toward first period. The silence is awkward. Then Alexis says, "Well thanks for keeping us out of it," Alexis says. "My parents would have totally lost it." Then I guess she feels bad because she looks at the ground and says, "I'm sorry about Cross-Country… and about Josh. But at least you weren't kicked off the team, right?" Now her voice sounds upbeat, like she's trying to find the bright side.

"Yeah," I say. But somehow, I'm not sure I'm going to get off that easy.

Coach Elsberry glances at me as I walk into history class, He manages a quick "Come see me after school" as I try to slip out at the end. He never even looks up as I acknowledge his words.

Later, when I push through the hall doors that lead to the gym, I'm surprised to see Josh sitting on the bench outside of Coach Elsberry's office waiting. His head is thrown back against the wall and he's staring at a spot where the top of the wall meets the ceiling. His long legs stretch out in front of him. I wait down the hall, hoping he won't see me. No such luck. He turns his head my way, closes his eyes, then turns back again. He resumes staring at the ceiling. I sit down on the next bench over. My knee bounces.

"Well, at least I don't have to face Elsberry alone." Josh's voice takes me by surprise. I look over at him. He doesn't sound angry, more resigned.

He glances at me and lets out a deep sigh.

I examine my shoes. I can't look at him. He probably hates me.

The door to the boys' locker room opens and Coach Elsberry rushes through, followed by a powerful whiff of locker room air. He looks at us and unlocks his office door. "Inside," he says, waiting at the threshold for us to go in ahead of him.

Coach Elsberry doesn't yell. He sits at his desk and examines his fingernails while we stand, waiting on the other side.

"Phillips wants me to replace you as team captain, son. I hate to have to say it, but he's making quite a stink."

Josh stares over the coach's head. He stands there, like he deserves whatever happens.

Why doesn't he defend himself? He never even went in the gym.

Coach shakes his head again and runs his hand through his hair.

"I'm stumped," he says. "How could you be so irresponsible? You are supposed to set an example. You are applying to an independent high school this year. These kinds of things will be on your record, son. What on earth were you thinking?" He shakes his head again. "I haven't decided what I'm going to do yet. I have to think about it. But I swear, I'm stumped. Tyler Mays of all people."

"Coach, Josh didn't—"

He cuts me off. "Josh takes responsibility for his own actions. Isn't that right, Josh?"

"Yes, sir." Josh's voice sounds flat.

Coach looks at me. "And you." I cringe. He doesn't raise his voice, but the anger and disappointment are loud and clear. "Of all the…" He doesn't finish the sentence. "Let me say…" He stops, takes a breath, and starts again. "Don't think for one minute that I won't kick you off my team if anything like this happens again. I don't care what your times were in the last meet, or what medals you win." He looks at his lap as he tries to get control of himself. "Consider yourself warned."

Coach stands up, turns around to look at the wall calendar behind his desk. His muscles tense. After a minute, his shoulders drop, and he turns to face us again.

"Lucky for you two, the Northern Virginia Invitational is not for another three weeks. I fully expect you both to be in competitive shape despite your suspension from practice. Get your miles in on your own time. "You read me?"

"Yes, sir," Josh says. I nod when he turns to get my answer. "Now get out here. I have a practice to run."

Walking home after an hour of sitting in a stuffy detention classroom with nothing to do but homework, I feel like I am dragging an anchor.

How had things gotten so screwed up?

The thing that stings the most, though, is the empty sidewalk stretching in front of me as I round the corner of my street. There's no sign of my Battlefield Boy. I haven't seen him since I walked home with Josh last week.

You'd think I'd be relieved. So why does it feel like I've been punched in the stomach?

Jeremy

January 10, 1862

Blue's tail rapped the quilt next to Jeremy's leg, then the dog dropped to the floor beside the bed. His ears stood up, and he stared at the door to the cabin with his tongue hanging out. His tail swayed back and forth.

What is that dog up to now? Jeremy fought the desire to snuggle deeper into the quilt.

In the next moment, the cabin latch released, and Jeremy's blood raced to his chest. He leapt up, had his gun in an instant, and pressed his back against the wall next to the door, waiting.

Blue's tail waved quicker. Whoever it was, Blue knew him. The door opened wider, and Blue seemed to light up with a smile, moonlight glowed in his eyes, as he leaped straight in the air in front of the intruder's face.

"Hush, Blue," came a familiar voice, and a hand went out and stroked the dog's neck as the animal settled to the ground.

In the next moment, Pa stepped into the cabin and removed his hat. Jeremy put down his gun and stepped into the moonlight.

"Jeremy." Pa reached out and pulled him hard to his chest with one arm. Blue jumped and twisted in the air beside them.

Jeremy let Pa's arms engulf him. He buried his face in his father's shoulder. His familiar scent swept over him, smoke, sweat, and the outdoors. He'd been gone for so long. It felt like a miracle to have him standing there. Heavy hands patted Jeremy's back as he grabbed handfuls of Pa's coat, and he fought the choking sensation in his throat. They held each other for a moment, unable to let each other go. Blue poked his nose between them.

Pa's arms released him. Jeremy stepped back as Pa bent to pat Blue. "What are you doing here? How'd you get past the pickets?"

"I've been trying to make my way back here for weeks, Son. Rebel forces are everywhere. They're conscripting everyone who's got two legs and a gun." He looked up and his voice trailed off. He stared behind Jeremy. Ma stood in the doorway of their room. Her eyes glistened and her mouth was drawn into a tight line like she was trying not cry.

Three long strides carried Pa across the cabin, and he threw his arms around Ma, lifting her off her feet.

"You're back!" she said, her voice muffled by his coat.

Pa set her down and she put her hands on either side of his face, then pressed her mouth against his. "You're back!" she said again after a long kiss.

"I've missed you, Laurie. I've missed you so much." Pa's voice rung with joy, but something else sounded in Pa's voice that reminded Jeremy of when they'd buried the last baby. Blue danced circles in the cabin. His tail waving like a battle flag.

"Come," Ma said, taking Pa's hand.

"I heard from Mother that you were expecting a baby, but..."

Ma placed a tightly wrapped bundle into Pa's arms. He stared into Sarah's face as he settled into the rocking chair, wiping his hand under his nose.

Jeremy piled a log on the embers in the hearth. He wanted to hear everything about the war. He had a million questions.

"She's beautiful, Laurie. Did you name her for your Mother, like you wanted?"

Ma nodded. "She's strong, too, John." She smiled down at the baby. "Almost as big as Jeremy when he was born."

A look passed between his parents that Jeremy didn't understand. Her other babies had been small and weak. Ma busied herself with water for coffee and settled it on top of the iron rack just over the new flames that leapt from the log Jeremy had added to the hearth.

Orange light flickered on Pa's face. He looked thin. A thick tangle of hair fell down to his shoulders and covered one side of his face. Grey streaked the beard on his chin and at his temples.

"I can only stay a short while, Laurie." Pa looked down at Sarah. "With those pickets so close, they're bound to notice a man in the house. I can't risk being arrested." Ma didn't look at Pa as he continued. "If they don't hang me for shirking the muster call, they'll hang me for skedaddling North. I came to see you three. I missed you all something awful, but I can't stay."

He looked back at Ma. Her back was to them both when her shoulders slumped.

Jeremy broke the silence. "What's it like, Pa? Have ya shot any Rebels?

"Jeremy!" Ma turned and barked at him with a sharpness he hadn't heard since Sarah was born.

Pa looked at her then said, "This war is nasty business, Son. I won't speak of the things I've seen." He looked down at Sarah and was quiet. The fire crackled and when he looked up his voice cracked, and he sniffed. "How are you making out, Laurie?

"The winter will prove a long one, I'm afraid," she said. "We weren't able to lay in our usual stores." She sounded tired. Both Union and Confederate armies had marched back and forth across the area so many times, they had a few shovelfuls of corn to show for the summer's work. The first crop was trampled and the second and third stolen.

Ma turned back to the coffee pot. She stared into the fire. Pa rocked Sarah silently. After he finished his coffee, Pa glanced at Jeremy, then stood. "I got to go," he said.

Pa's eyes rested on Sarah who gurgled and squirmed, threatening to break into a full-on squall. He smiled as Ma rushed to take the baby from him. Jeremy dug his fingernail into the grain of the tabletop and worked it back and forth.

"Just come home safe," she said as she turned away to feed the baby.

"You're leaving?"

"I got to go before those pickets take notice, Son. I know you understand."

Jeremy understood. Ma would keep Jeremy out of the fighting. Well, the moment she mentioned heading North, he would follow Pa. That was certain

17

CHARLOTTE

JOSH WALKS INTO DETENTION A MINUTE OR SO AFTER me on Wednesday afternoon. He walks down the aisle, nods at me, and sits down in the next row. We wait for the Detention Monitor, Ms. Green, to arrive. Kids lounge on the desks. Boys bump shoulders and greet each other with complex hand gestures, calling each other names that I don't think were the ones their parents gave them. Some speak Spanish. It's like they're all at a party or something.

When Eric Finson struts in, everyone cheers, and he knocks knuckles as he walks down the aisle.

"Big crowd for a Wednesday," he says. A few kids in front chuckle. Eric rolls through the room like a celebrity then slides into the seat directly next to me. He scratches his chin, removes his baseball cap, and puts it on backwards. He looks around and then taps me on the shoulder.

"Hey, Dude. What are you in for? Aren't you supposed to be out running in circles or something? That would be punish-ment enough for me." He seems impressed with his own wit, but no one else appreciates the joke. I don't have any idea how he knows I'm on the Cross Country team.

Josh swings around and stares at Eric. "Hey, man, leave her alone," he says. "She's not an accomplished delinquent yet. Maybe you can give her a few pointers."

Eric looks like he has something to say to that, but at that moment, Ms. Green enters the room.

"Take out your work, people. I want absolute silence in here. I have a stack of papers to grade. Grading papers always makes me mean. Do not test me today."

Books and computers come out of backpacks, and papers rustle, until the room settles into a forced silence. My leg bounces under the desk.

When Ms. Green finally stands up and opens the door, I leap out of my chair, swing my backpack on my shoulder, and hit Eric Finson right in the face.

"Whoa, watch what you do with that thing," he says. I know I should apologize but I have to get out of here. Every inch of my body aches to move. The aisle in front of me is clogged with kids. I'm stuck behind a clump of girls blocking my way

From the next aisle over, I hear Josh. "Some of us are better at wasting time than others," he says.

"Gotta pace yourself, Dude," Eric says. "It comes with experience, man. She'll be chillin' with the best of us in no time, I guarantee it."

Eric lifts himself over the desk and walks out next to Josh. They fall into an easy rhythm as they head into the hall in front of me.

"So, what's up with you, Josh?" Eric asks. "What you do to earn a stretch in the Green Room?"

He smiles and they look back at me. "Actually, I guess you could say we were in the wrong place at the wrong time," Josh says. "Bad luck."

As they saunter down the hall, I race past them to my locker. When I burst through the school's front doors a couple of minutes later, Josh and Eric are sitting on the boulders, talking like two old men on a park bench. I hurry down the driveway.

"Hey, man, who's your friend?" Eric asks Josh as I get closer. "She new?"

Josh opens his mouth to say something, then he stops. He looks from me to Eric and says, "Charlotte Cross, allow me to introduce you to my friend, Eric Finson. Eric, meet Charlotte Cross. She sees ghosts."

Jeremy

February 15, 1862

Jeremy trudged up the hill toward home with a brace of two scrawny rabbits slung over his shoulders. His face felt like a solid block of ice and he couldn't feel his fingers as he waded through knee deep piles of leaves. This stretch of trees was all that was left of the forest that had covered the hill down to the river. There was no need to worry about scaring game. Hunting by the falls had never been so paltry.

Soldiers from both sides cleared every twig for acres for firewood. They had taken fence rails, and even started in on dismantling the chicken coop. Not that it mattered. There weren't any chickens left. Ma had managed to rescue one of the good layers, so they had an egg or two in the morning. Now that hen strutted around in the cabin like she owned the place. But the rooster and other chickens disappeared pretty quickly after Christmas.

Above Jeremy's head, the wind stirred the branches of the last trees. The trail to the river seemed like the only place he'd been lately that wasn't a sea of white tents. Trotting ahead of him, Blue examined every trunk. Clouds of breath hung in front of them both. When Jeremy closed his eyes, the rush of wa-ter over the falls behind him made his heart ache for all that had changed.

Jeremy climbed the hill that marked the end of their land and stared across a long expanse of jagged stumps. Blue sniffed one, then lifted his leg to mark it.

"That a boy, Blue. Make it nice and strong. You make sure everyone knows this is our land."

The wind carried a strange moaning sound from up ahead. Jeremy and Blue stopped at the same moment and listened. The moan separated into the frantic grunts of a cow mooing.

Annabelle! She sounded like she was being chased. Jeremy

bolted forward. So far, they'd been lucky. All their neighbors' stock had been stolen. But Annabelle's ribs stuck out so much lately, it hurt to milk her. She hardly looked worth the trouble to steal.

When Blue reached the edge of the pasture, he tore off out of sight. Jeremy struggled over roots and through the mud. The mooing stopped suddenly. But now Blue's barking competed with the sound of Jeremy's heart in his ears and a howl of the wind.

Cold fear crept up his back and into his shoulders as he crested the hill.

Annabelle lay on the ground, her head at an odd angle. Blue barked and growled as two soldiers in shabby gray uniforms kicked and swatted at him with their guns. The butt of one gun connected, and Blue yelped. He flew sideways landing on the ground. A scream rose in Jeremy's throat that he couldn't stifle. Blue was up again. He shook himself and lunged at the man who had turned back toward Annabelle. The dog grabbed hold of the man's arm with his jaw. Annabelle, Jeremy could see now, struggled to get up, but her legs weren't moving right. They had hobbled her. She moved her legs and neck toward each other, and her sides rose and fell in quick bursts of shallow breathing.

She's still alive.

"Stop!" Jeremy's shout was swallowed by the wind.

He ran closer. "Stop!" he shouted again. This time the man

kneeling by Annabelle's head looked up. He didn't pay Jeremy any attention. Jeremy was still too far to shoot the Rebel. The damn gun wasn't loaded, anyway. He threw it to the ground, tossing the rabbits with it, then stumbled forward. As he ran, he watched the soldier place a hand against Annabelle's neck. The glint of a knife blade flashed. Jeremy pushed himself into a run. Blue pulled the other man's arm.

"No!" he shouted.

Not Annabelle.

The man with the knife jerked his arm and blood spurted. The cow's head and legs dropped. Jeremy ran a few more steps, then fell to his knees.

"Nooooooo!"

Blue heard him. He released the other soldier who fell back against Annabelle's stomach. They'd killed her! Jeremy raised his hands to his face, then doubled over and pounded the ground. A seething anger swelled in his chest.

Blue was there, nudging his arm with his nose.

He pounded the ground again.

They had no right!

18

CHARLOTTE

"JOSH!" WHAT IS HE DOING?

Eric's face changes instantly. His eyes slide to the side, and he smiles. "I should have known, man. You definitely have an aura."

"Relax, Charlotte." Josh steps up next to me. "Eric's mother is a palm reader. She owns the shop in the old strip. You know the one. 'Madame Finson, Palm Reader, Medium, and Advisor.'"

I can't believe what I'm hearing. Is he making fun of me? I look back and forth from Eric to Josh. I shrink.

"So, what kind of problem are you having?" Eric sounds all business now. "I have some experience with these things."

"Go on, Charlotte, tell him," Josh says. "He's not kidding. Eric's a friend of mine. We went to grade school together. He lives on my block." I must look pretty upset because now Josh steps closer to Eric and nudges him with his elbow. "Tell her what a medium is, Eric. Quick, before she tears my head off."

Eric sways slightly. "Hey, man, you guys got a problem with a ghost, I can help. The other stuff between you two, you have to see my sister about. Relationship issues are her department. Ma says she has a gift." My face goes hot. "Now, if it's ghosts you're dealing with, I'm your guy."

"You believe in ghosts?" I'm still not convinced they aren't making fun of me.

"I've been known to handle a problem spirit or two." Eric shifts. "I do prefer the less belligerent ones. You got one mad at you for some reason?"

Can he be for real? Of course, I'm the one *talking* to a ghost.

"I have a sudden craving for a chocolate shake," Josh cuts in. "Why don't you tell Eric all about your friend while we walk to McDonald's."

By the time we're sipping shakes in a booth at the back of the fast food joint, I've told Eric the entire story, about the YouTube video, about the twig, and about Dad and Afghanistan. As the story spills out, a pain grows inside my chest. I sit across from Eric, feeling more and more confused, desperate to stay in control. I push away the question that's been nagging me that I haven't wanted to think about.

If ghosts are for real, where's Dad?

Eric scratches his chin. He thinks for a moment, then says, "Interesting. Let me think about this for a minute." I focus on the fact that both Josh and Eric are serious.

Eric gets a look on his face like he's about to solve all my problems.

"Since you're already talking to this ghost, you don't need

my help. This ghost, Jeremy you say he's called? It doesn't sound like you're afraid of him. Right?"

I shake my head.

"A lot of times a ghost doesn't know what to do."

"What, like following the light, or something?" Josh asks.

"Possibly," Eric says. He seems so different from the kid who walked into the assembly the first day of school. "Sometimes, though, it's the living who keep the dead from crossing over," he says. "Sometimes a spirit hangs around because they left some mess behind that they need to clean up. Ma says it's complicated." Eric pauses for a moment. I feel his eyes on me.

"Maybe you need to help him find out what's keeping him here."

I gnaw on the cuticle of my right thumb. "How do we do that?" I ask.

"Ask him," Eric says.

"You're the man, Eric," Josh says as he leans across the booth and hold his fist out to Eric.

"No sweat," Eric says as he bumps Josh's fist. "Glad to be of service."

Josh leans back in the booth beside me looking like he has just solved the biggest problem in the universe. He smiles and nods. "What did I tell you, Charlotte?" Josh points at Eric. "He's your man," he says, laughing

While they bump fists and congratulate each other, I lay my head on the seat. "It's worth a try, I guess," I say, wishing I felt as confident and calm as they sound.

Jeremy

The grey clouds reflected in the glass of the Turner cabin windows as if the house wore a shroud. Ginny picked up her pace as she turned into the lane leading to the stable. Jeremy gave the horse some rein but steered her close to the cabin steps. Since Annabelle was gone, he hated going into the barn. It felt so empty.

The pickets who were camped by the front gate when Ma and he left this morning were nowhere to be seen, now. At least they wouldn't have to show a pass just to get down the lane to their own home.

"Where'd those dang soldiers go?" Jeremy wanted to keep an eye on them. It made him jumpy when he didn't know where they were. "The lines change all the time. I'm sure they'll be back." Ma sure did seem to know a lot about the army for someone who was a pacifist.

"You unload the boxes, Jeremy," Ma said, as she slowly dismounted from the wagon. "After I get Sarah inside, I'll unhitch Ginny."

Sarah stirred in the box he'd anchored with rope behind the bench. "It'll give me pleasure to walk her in the pasture after that long trip."

Ma touched her back and stared out over the barren field.

Thunder rumbled overhead and a fat drop of rain plopped on the dust in front of him.

Jeremy hoisted a crate up onto his shoulder then removed the musket from under the buckboard's bench. He was low on gunpowder. He couldn't risk getting the gun wet. He headed up the cabin steps, then stopped. The door stood slightly ajar. Jeremy's chest tightened like he'd been snared by a rope, and his breathing went shallow. He'd latched that door. Nothing was more certain. Someone had been in the cabin.

He stepped away from the door and lowered the crate to the ground. Blue sniffed at the black crack in the open doorway. The dog stepped back and lowered his head with one paw raised. The fur between his shoulders ruffled as a low growl rose in his throat. Jeremy's heart pumped. He had to think. Whoever opened that door was still inside.

"Hush, Blue. Get over here." The dog obeyed and stood waiting for directions at Jeremy's side. The scoundrel had heard Blue growl, no doubt about it.

Dang dog, he'd lost whatever surprise they'd had.

"Don't be so surly, I'll feed you as soon as I get these boxes unpacked," he said to cover for the dog's mistake.

Jeremy turned away from the open door, checked the gun's packing, then eyed the cabin's windows. Something moved beyond the glass.

Jeremy walked along the front wall of the house, slid next

to a side window and peered into the darkness. A man in a blue coat stood beside the door at the foot of Jeremy's bed. A deserter.

The man's back was to Jeremy as he looked through the space between the door jamb and the door. Jeremy's scalp pricked. The man's leg, visible through torn trousers, oozed blood. Blood smeared his face, pants, and hands.

Jeremy crept back to the front porch, laid his gun on the wooden floor panels, and silently pushed himself up onto the deck. Flat against the cabin wall he could not be seen from inside.

Ma moved toward the steps carrying Sarah. Jeremy's heart seemed to have found a new rhythm as a prickle of panic rose from his feet right up to his scalp. He took short shallow breaths as Ma looked into the cabin door and froze. The tip of a gun barrel emerged through the door, aimed right at Ma and Sarah.

"Where'd that boy of yours get to, Ma'am? I saw him take the gun out of the wagon. You tell him to come out of hiding wherever he is, or I'll shoot. You know I will." Ma's eyes shifted slightly toward Jeremy who raised his own gun. He squinted, aiming across the barrel.

The soldier's gun barrel jerked forward as he stepped through the doorway. The soldier stumbled, favoring his bad leg, and he turned toward Jeremy. Their eyes met. Panic raised the hair on Jeremy's neck as the man swung his gun back aiming at Ma and the baby. A large black mole on the soldier's cheek stood out against his pale skin, and his uniform hung loose from his boney shoulders. Jeremy could smell the woods on the man, like he hadn't been inside for weeks.

"Don't make no trouble, boy. I don't want no trouble."

He hobbled a step closer to Ma, keeping his eye on Jeremy. Jeremy stopped breathing. As long as the soldier stood so close to Ma and Sarah, there was nothing Jeremy could do.

The butt of his gun felt hard against Jeremy's shoulder and heavy in his hands. Blue gingerly took a step forward, as if he were walking on his toes. The dog's entire body shook as if ready to pounce. A growl rumbled in his throat.

The soldier spun on his good leg throwing him off balance. The gun came around aimed at Blue. Then, quickly, he turned it back on Ma.

Blue's growl grew louder, and he curled his upper lip exposing pointy teeth. "There's no need to make this difficult, son." The man moved closer to Ma. "Lower your weapon now and call off that dog. We all want to walk away from this alive."

Another low rumble came out of Blue, and the man's eyes shifted to the dog. The barrel of the Rebel's gun, pointed directly at Ma, no more than two feet away. He watched Blue. The dog snarled, teeth glistening, his ears flat. The man stepped down one stair, even closer to Ma. His eyes never leaving Blue. The dog snarled again. Now the soldier swung his gun back at Blue. Time slowed down. The soldier's finger trembled as he began to squeeze the trigger on his gun, and before he could think, Jeremy fired. A deafening blast roared in his ears, the gun's butt kicked his shoulder, as the man flew backwards across the cabin porch. Sulfur stung in Jeremy's eyes and nose.

Sarah screamed. Ma lay on her back clutching the baby. Jeremy's heart leaped into his throat, pounding at a frantic pace. Ma was on the ground. He raced to her as Blue pounced at the man, feet on his chest, nose pointing, waiting for him to move.

"Ma? Ma?" Jeremy's voice sounded far away. The blast echoed in his ear. "Are you hit? Ma?" His hands shook. "I had to shoot."

Why didn't she answer him?

Ma's eyes fluttered. She looked up at Jeremy and gasped. He looked at her dress and patted her arms with one hand. The other, still shaking, held the gun. A streak of red stretched across her skirt. But the dress wasn't torn. It wasn't her blood. Sarah's hoarse scream turned to a raspy, desperate wail.

The soldier, lying in the dirt, released a gasping gurgle, his face a smear of blue and red. A splatter of black stretched from the man's head toward Ma. Jeremy stood up and kicked the soldier's gun away from his body. The intruder's leg twitched. Then he lay still.

Ma sat up and touched her forehead with the back of her hand. Her eyes settled on the pulpy mass of flesh that had been the man's face. She patted Sarah.

"Help me up," she said and held out her hand for Jeremy. He pulled her to standing. She pulled him close to her and wrapped her free arm around him. Her whole body trembled.

Jeremy's shoulders released as if they'd been untied. He breathed in her familiar scent of lye soap.

In the next moment she released him. Ma took a deep breath then turned her attention to Sarah, stiff and screaming. She grasped her to her heart. The rain was coming down harder now.

"Shhhh. There now. You just had a bad fright. It'll be alright. Shhhhhh." Ma patted Sarah's back and bounced as she hurried inside. She looked at Jeremy from the corner of her eye as she comforted Sarah.

"I thought he'd shoot thee," she said from the cabin door. "I never expected..." She stopped. Jeremy was shaking out of control. She pulled him up the stairs out of the rain and gave him another tight hug with her free arm.

As Sarah's cries slowed to hiccupping gasps, Ma turned toward the fallen soldier shaking her head. "Best move him into the barn. Tomorrow, we'll take him into town and explain what happened to the authorities."

Jeremy stared at the man on the ground. A creeping dread spread through him. Ma walked inside. Jeremy stared at her back.

She aimed to turn him in.

He watched her close the cabin door, then Jeremy grabbed the dead man by his boots and dragged him toward the barn with a hard, hot knot growing in his stomach. A trail of black smeared the ground behind him and mixed with mud. The dang fool was about to shoot Ma. Somehow, he didn't think that would matter to the Union commander.

There was a dead solider lying in his yard, and he had killed him.

19

CHARLOTTE

TWO DAYS LATER, I RUN THE FAMILIAR PATH ALONG the eastern rim of Manassas Battlefield. Beau trots at my side. I have to find my battlefield friend. I haven't seen him since Josh and I ran away from him.

I've missed him.

The evening light slants low, making me squint. And then I'm charging up the hill. My heart pumps furiously, but not from the run.

I hope this works. If he really is a ghost, I need to help him.

I crest the hill and slow to a walk. Beau pulls me straight for the water fountain. Worry pierces me in the chest.

Jeremy's not here.

I turn the nozzle and water springs in a long arch over the side of the shiny metal basin.

Beau turns his head sideways and laps at the stream. Then sweet, cold water slides down my throat. I draw in another mouthful of water, stand up, and swallow.

With my heart thundering in my ears, I step around the corner of the building.

A wind rolls through the tops of the trees that line the

battlefield in front of me carrying the faint smell of gunpowder and then, there he is, like he's been waiting for me.

Poor guy. He looks so lonely.

I step toward him, but not Beau. He lunges, dragging me along, prancing joyfully. His tongue lolls out of his mouth. Jeremy's sad smile tugs at my heart.

"Blue!" he reaches down and pats my dog who sits quietly beside Jeremy, panting. I stroke Beau's back. Jeremy is so close, I can smell the mud and grass stains on his knees. And the gunpowder.

How can he be a ghost? He's so real. And solid.

"I was worried I wouldn't see you again," I say.

Jeremy shrugs. "Most folks don't take no notice of me," he says.

"I want to help," I say it before I lose my nerve.

He looks across the battlefield. "No one can help me," he says.

"I can try," I say, more determined now.

"Nope," he says. "Ma won't ever forgive me."

"Why?" I ask. "What happened?"

He looks at me sideways. "She didn't want me to join up. She thinks war's a sin."

"You were in a war?"

"Our farm was on the Potomac." He says the river's name funny, like it rhymes with automat. "Above the falls. Pa was fighting for Lincoln. I lied, and they gave me a gun and a uniform."

Lincoln?

My throat aches making it difficult to speak. He's been alone for over 170 years. Since… the Civil War.

"Ma dosn't know where I ran to. Or what happened to me."

"Tell me her name, or your father's name, and I'll find them, Jeremy," I say. "I promise."

Jeremy pats Beau's back and shakes his head.

John and Laurie Turner," he says and then he vanishes.

Jeremy

April 22, 1862

If he was going, he had to go. Now. He had waited too long already, and it would be light soon.

Ma had taken forever to go to bed. Sarah fussed more than usual. Her coughing rattled through the darkness. Maybe she was getting sick.

Blue snored on the hearth. Jeremy forced the lump in his throat down, as he pressed on the latch. He couldn't risk waking the dog.

He felt like he was drowning. It wasn't like he had a choice about leaving. She aimed to turn over the body of the dead soldier to the Union commander in town. When she did, Jeremy would have to answer for murder.

The fire crackled as a glowing ember flared and a stick of wood shifted. Jeremy's heart nearly leapt out onto the floor. He listened for movement in the darkness. With a sudden determination, he held his breath and pulled open the door. The hinges complained with a low-pitched whine. Jeremy froze. If Blue woke, he'd never get away.

Where Jeremy was going, he couldn't take Blue.

He squeezed through the small crack between the door and its frame. As he turned to pull the door closed, Blue appeared behind him. The dog pushed his nose through the opening.

"No, Blue," Jeremy whispered. "Lay down." Blue looked up at him. The dog's head shifted, and the moonlight reflected in his eyes like on the surface of a black lake, but he didn't move. A whine rose in his throat.

"Hush! You'll wake Ma." Jeremy froze. "You can't come, Blue. You got to stay here and take care of Ma and Sarah." Jeremy's voice cracked as he spoke the last words. Blue scratched the floor in the opening.

Why wouldn't the dog obey?

Jeremy turned to look at the sky, then hung his head. "I got to go, Blue. I can't take you with me." The dog stepped back as Jeremy closed the door behind him, then Blue barked a quick sharp yelp.

"Damn, Blue." Jeremy jumped off the porch without touching the steps. The moon peaked through the branches of the last remaining tree on the lane. Stumps of what had been the woods filled the landscape in front of him like so many tombstones in a cemetery.

Blue barked again, louder. Jeremy ran toward the barn. He had to get out of sight before Ma woke up. Jeremy's moonlight shadow raced ahead of him. With his breath coming in quick bursts, he sprinted across the barren field that had been their cornfield. He rounded the corner of the barn, stopped short and listened. He heard only the quiet voices of the pickets somewhere beyond the hedge and the thunder of the falls. Inside the barn, Ginny slept. Ginny and the dead soldier. A shudder crept up his back. Then shame swept through him at the memory of other soldiers slitting Annabelle's throat. Those men carved her up right in front of him. Her carcass had lain there for days before he had the strength to move what was left of her. Blue had sat a respectful distance away, like Annabelle's honor guard. That dead soldier in the barn might not have been the one who did it, but as far as he was concerned, he deserved what he got.

"Jeremy?" He raised his head. Ma called softly from the cabin porch. Blue barked again. If he kept it up, he'd get those soldiers curious and then it would be over. She'd tell them about what had happened, and they'd take him into town and try him for murder.

Keeping the barn between him and the cabin door, Jeremy broke into a run. Ma wouldn't leave Sarah alone inside. Maybe she'd think he just went to the privy. Blue had known he was leaving. That's why he barked. By the time Ma realized it too, he'd be too far to hear her calling.

The moon grew blurry momentarily as he fought the growing pain in his throat, then he dropped over the rise that led toward the river.

It was her fault that he had to go.

20

CHARLOTTE

I STARE AT THE MAILBOX NAILED TO THE WOODEN POST and the hand painted numbers. Yep, this is the right place, alright. But this is not at all what I expected. Beyond the half wire, half wood-post fence a dilapidated house looms over a yard of sparse grass and weeds.

Finding Jeremy's address had been a little tricky, but I found a John enlisted in a Pennsylvania regiment, and Laurie Turner listed on a directory of Virginia Friends communities online. But she had been expelled. She was a Quaker.

Their hometown: Vienna, Virginia. Jeremy had grown up a couple miles up the Pike from the Manassas Battlefield.

On the website, it was easy to trace birth and death records of all the Turners, except for Jeremy. No date of death had been recorded. From the official state records, it's like he never died. The house in front of us was the address listed for his last surviving relative, Elanor St. John Cooper. And from the look of it, the last time the house had been painted was sometime in around the Civil War. In the middle of a batch of newer homes, this one was an antique.

Weeds grow between loose red bricks that might be a

walkway, but it stops about four feet from a set of crumbling concrete risers leading up to a porch. Even though shutters hang crooked, and the siding looks rotten, the house seems proud, somehow, like once it was grand and elegant.

Four tall pillars and a double front door give it a kind of Old South feel. A dirt path leads from the gate through the sparse grass along the side of the house and disappears in the back yard. I stand looking at the front door.

"Should we ring the doorbell?" Eric asks.

"What do we have to lose?" Josh asks. We drop our bikes on the grass by the fence.

I turn toward the house. No use putting it off. The old gate groans as I push it open. Josh and Eric follow me.

At the foot of the crumbling front stairs, I change my mind. "Let's see what's around back."

The side yard and back garden are almost as bad as the front, but a deck stretches along the back of the house. The stairs up seem a little sturdier.

Standing like a sentinel next to the door, a rocking chair creaks in a breeze that carries the strong scent of begonias. A thin seat cushion covered in a bright red flower pattern rests on the seat, and a red shawl hangs over the back. On the other side of the door, a table is stacked high with empty flowerpots and baskets. A second rocking chair rocks in the same breeze, its cushion spouting stuffing. At the far end, on a porch swing lays an orange cat, sound asleep.

"Sounds like somebody's home," Josh says. Piano music drifts through the screen door that's hanging slightly ajar.

"Go ahead, knock," Eric says.

"Might as well." I give the screen door three quick raps. We wait, then I call into the darkness beyond the door. "Hello?"

The cat on the swing, lifts its head dreamily, looks at us, and after a moment's thought, stands up, raises its back legs into a long lazy stretch, then sits down demurely, ready to receive guests.

We wait. Nothing.

"Hello?" I call again and knock louder.

This time, from somewhere inside comes a booming bark, the scrambling of claws on wood, and the distinct sound of a dog hurrying down the stairs.

"Oh hush, Colonel, I hear it," shouts a voice a moment later. It's a woman's voice, crinkled with age, but lively also.

"Coming," she sings. The clack of claws on wooden floors gets louder. It sounds like the dog and the woman are racing each other to the door.

I laugh at the droopy-faced hound dog who slides up to the screen. A couple seconds behind him is a thin older woman, strands of grey hair falling out of the tight knot at the back of her head. Her face, though crisscrossed with lines, is bright and smiling. Large button earrings match her blue cardigan which is draped around her shoulders and clasped by a chain. A white blouse is tucked into a worn pair of jeans which are stuffed in turn into a pair of green rubber boots. In one hand she holds a bucket, in the other, a long thin artist's paint brush. She looks out the screen door, blinks, and says, "Oh my! Well, you aren't at all who I expected."

After a brief introduction that leaves out the reasons for our visit, we sit in the porch chairs. Our host, Mrs. Eleanor St. John Cooper—Lily she insists we call her—rocks in the rocker. Amber, the orange cat, is curled up in Josh's lap as if he has been waiting all day for the chance.

Lily takes a sip of her tea which she has retrieved from inside, and says, "So you're interested in the Turner family, then?"

"Yes," I say, then guilt makes me confess. "Well, not exactly. It's kind of a long story."

"I say start at the beginning, and the story will tell itself," Lily says. "It's funny how much you find out when you just set it going."

I look to Eric and Josh for help. They smile. They're going to be no help at all.

"I'm actually interested in one person in particular. Jeremy Turner? Do you know anything about him?"

Lily's face softens. "Now why in the world would you ask about him?" Her voice has lost some of its brightness.

"It's just that..."

"Jeremy Turner was my great-grandmother's only brother. He disappeared about the time of the war between the states."

Lily pauses for a moment, then says, "I am Jeremy Turner's only kin that I know of. Of course, he may have other relatives wherever he ran off to. What happened to him has always been one of the family's great mysteries." Lily pauses again and looks out into the field behind the house. Her expression seems sad all of a sudden, like we've awakened a bad memory.

I look to Eric and Josh again. Still, I get nothing.

Lily doesn't wait.

"My grandmother said her mother stood at the gate every evening staring down the lane. Her mother, my great-grandmother, waited there every night until the day she died, like she expected him home any minute."

A deep sadness creeps into Lily's voice. Her wide blue eyes remind me of Jeremy's. I shiver. There is no denying it. Jeremy has got to be Lily's long-lost great-uncle.

"They're all buried down behind the old shed," she continues. "That's one of the reasons I never could bring myself to sell the place. My whole family's bones are buried just over the hill there." Lily pauses and raises her eyes to the distance again. For a moment, she seems to have forgotten all about us.

"You don't know what a comfort that is." Then she startles and looks at us "How in heaven's name did you hear about that missing boy?"

JEREMY

April 24, 1862 Rural Pennsylvania

"Papers." The seated man didn't look up when Jeremy reached the front of the line. "Don't got any," Jeremy said.

Now the recruiter squinted up at him and sat back. "Date of birth?"

Sweat trickled down Jeremy's neck. "October 14th, 1847. I'm 15 years old, sir." The officer in a blue uniform and tight beard scrutinized him.

"You're not 16, yet? Can anyone here verify who you are?"

Jeremy had walked for two days and nights, freezing in the winter cold. He had dodged Confederate lookouts and then waded across the river where he knew it was at its lowest, swimming though swells and over rocks. Then he hid from Union sentries as he crossed Maryland. Now in Pennsylvania, his stomach gnawed at his ribs. All he had eaten since his last dinner with Ma was the piece of bread he had stuffed in his pocket before he left. He couldn't take much. Ma would need it.

By now, she had probably figured out that he had run. Why did she have to turn him in? She'd be dead if he hadn't shot that dang deserter. And Blue, too.

Jeremy hugged himself tightly and blew on his hands. "No,

Sir, but I got my own hunting gun, and I can hit a rabbit as well as anybody at 100 paces." Jeremy's eyes met the recruiters.

"So, you want to shoot yourself a couple of Rebels?"

"Yes, sir. Been shooting buck and coyote since I could walk. I shoot straight enough to hit a traitor, I expect. Doesn't that make me qualified for the army?"

A laugh rose from the men in the line. Jeremy allowed himself a small smile. The recruiter puffed out his cheeks.

"Buck and coyote don't shoot back, son. "We can't take anyone under eighteen without their parent's approval. I expect your daddy is off fighting."

"Yes, sir."

"I'm afraid you're going to have get permission from your parents before you can enlist. Does your momma even know you're here, boy?"

The words sent heat rising up Jeremy's neck and cheeks and all his limbs suddenly felt heavy.

"You'll have to bring your momma or daddy to sign the papers before you can serve. Sorry, son. Go on home and ask your momma. Next." The man behind Jeremy stepped around him and placed a single sheet of paper on the desk in front of the recruiter.

Stung, Jeremy swallowed, turned on his heel, and headed across the street to where a group of men sat close to a wood stove. His stomach growled. He hadn't froze for three days, not eating or sleeping along the way to be turned away now. He looked around the busy town. No one was paying him any at-tention. There had to be something he could do. You'da thought they'd be begging for folks to shoot Rebels. He leaned against the trunk of a gnarled old elm tree. He'd find a way, even if he had to lie and cheat himself into the war.

21

CHARLOTTE

Before we can answer, Lily holds up a hand.

"Will you look at me, I've been blabbing on, I haven't even offered you anything to drink. Can I get you folks a soda?"

"No thank you. We were hoping you could tell us about Jeremy."

"Well..." Lily sighs like she knows she has to answer my questions sooner or later. "Let me see now." She looks out across the yard. "The Turner family owned a farm here and built the original home on the property. It wasn't much of a house, actually. More like a cabin."

Lilly points to the shed in the field not far from the house. "We still store the farm equipment there. Not that we use any of it anymore. We stopped planting back in the 70s. What with the cost of the land and the price of produce, it hardly seemed worth the effort. My husband and I sold off most of the land. They've put in quite a few homes since then."

When Jeremy lived here, this had all been farmland.

Eric interrupts Lily's talk about farm prices and land sales. He's so polite, I can't believe he's the same kid who got detention the first day of school. "Excuse me, Ma'am, would you mind if we take a look at that old shed?"

"Of course, help yourselves," Lilly rocks faster in her rocker. "When I was a girl, I loved climbing around that old attic. It was full of old trunks and things from my grandmother's day. Be careful, though. It's dark and the boards are old."

Eric starts to shake his head as we get closer to the shed. A collapsed ramp lies at the entrance to the cabin door.

"Dude, I am not going in there," he says.

"What are you talking about, man. It was your idea."

"Nah, you go ahead. I'll wait out here. Ghosts are one thing. But snakes. And spiders! No way, man."

I push the door open. It sticks then releases and a shower of dust rains down from overhead. After a couple of seconds, the dust clears, and we take a small step inside. No little light penetrates the dirt and cobwebs that cake the windows. It's nearly impossible to see.

The strip of light from the open door falls across piles of boxes, stacked to the ceiling. Scattered across the floor are pitchforks, long handled hoes, and the remains of something that looks like it might have been a tractor. A layer of dust softens the edges of everything and rises in clouds as I step into the silence. No one has been in here in a long time.

A second room at the other end of the main room is filled with collapsed furniture and more farm equipment. Piled in the corner, a stack of chairs with legs pointing up looks like a furry, eight-legged monster. Another chair lays on its side.

"Where do we start?" I look around. This isn't what I expected we'd be doing.

"Jeremy died in the 1800s." Eric calls to us from outside. "Look for the really old stuff." "And where would that be?" I whisper.

Josh shrugs. He looks around. "We don't even know what we're looking for," he says.

Just then Eric appears in the doorway. "Look for something Jeremy might recognize, a teapot or a toy," he says.

"It's hopeless. There isn't anything in here that would have been around when Jeremy was alive."

"Try the attic," Eric says.

Josh shrugs. We squint into the darkness above our heads. Lily did say she played in the attic where her grandmother's stuff was stored.

I step over piles of wood and boxes that have fallen and split open. As I get further into the cabin, my eyes begin to adjust to the dark. By the back wall, a ladder stretches up into shadow. I test a rung with my foot. It holds, so I start up.

This is nuts!

The low roof forces us both to bend over to keep from hitting our heads. Josh opens the shutters on the small window just under the eaves at the far end. A ray of light falls on the leaves and clutter that covers the floor. Dust floats thick in the light's path.

A large pile of boxes sits separate from the other things. I push away cobwebs.

This pile seems different than the others. A coarse rope wraps around a trunk made of sturdy board. It looks ancient. I run my hand along the top and dust rises in a cloud around us.

"This hasn't been opened in forever."

We clear a spot on the wooden floor and by the time we loosen the ropes my hands are shaking.

The smell of musty clothes drifts up from ancient fabrics. Lying on top is a delicate white baby's gown.

"What is all this stuff?" Josh asks.

"Things someone loved once." Beneath the top layers of clothes is a stack of papers, folded and tied together with a black ribbon.

Letters.

Josh pulls the bundle out and with the crinkle of old paper and begins to read. I sort through the clothes. A few layers farther down, there's a patchwork quilt, folded and wrapped in translucent paper. The corner patch has something embroidered on it.

"Josh," I say. "Look."

In minute cross stitch, someone has embroidered a baby's cradle and next to it, the words "Jeremy Michael Turner, October 14, 1847."

Jeremy

Shivering and slumped against the trunk of the giant elm, Jeremy stewed. He had to find Pa. He was sure he would sign the papers to let him enlist if he explained how Ma had wanted to turn in him, for shooting a deserter.

"Won't let you sign up, son?" A rough voice startled him, and Jeremy scrambled to his feet.

"Don't get all jumpy on me, boy. I'm just making conversation." The pot-bellied man in front of Jeremy was leaning on a weathered branch, using it like a crutch. Jeremy couldn't see the man's face. It was wrapped in a thick scarf, but he could see that he held his right leg off the ground and that the foot was bandaged.

"I ain't jumpy," Jeremy grumbled. "Didn't see you coming, that's all."

"I have a boy about your age." He studied Jeremy. "Looks to me like you've been traveling ruff. Tell me your name, son."

"Jeremy Turner."

"Well Jeremy Turner, I imagine you wouldn't turn your nose up at a plate of stew and a warm fire. Come with me, and I'll see if I can't help you out with that recruiter."

Jeremy swallowed. He certainly could use a meal. He'd

listen to what this old man had to say. Maybe he knew the recruiter. Or maybe he could help him find Pa.

The two walked to Betsy's Boarding House a few doors down from the old elm, where the man bought Jeremy a bowl of thin stew of potatoes and some kind of meat Jeremy couldn't identify. After he finished shoveling it into his stomach, Jeremy told the man, Bartholomew Crouch was his name, his story, from the moment Pa left, to the butchering of Annabelle, to Ma's threat to turn him in as he dragged the dead soldier into the barn. After a long silence, Crouch finally spoke.

"That's quite a tale, my boy. Quite a tale. It sounds to me like Lincoln could use a brave lad like yourself."

"But the army recruiter…

"Never mind what that recruiter said," Crouch interrupted. "Seems to me that if a fine young man wants to fight, the army ought to let him, Am I right?"

Jeremy eyed the stranger as the man went on talking. "I've been watching these recruiters for a couple of days. Don't move around too much with this bad leg of mine." He shifted in his chair moving his wounded leg out from under the table.

"I have a proposal for you, Jeremy Turner," he said finally. "Let's get another bowl of Betsy's fine stew in you, and then we'll go talk to that recruiter again."

By the time Jeremy and Mr. Crouch reached the head of the line, the sun had fallen behind the line of buildings along the street. Keeping his head low, Jeremy prepared to get another rebuke, but a new recruiter sat at the table at the end of the line.

"Next," the soldier in Union Blues snapped.

Crouch and Jeremy stepped up. The recruiter squinted at them.

"Good afternoon, sir. My name is Bartholomew Crouch," Crouch said, "I hear Lincoln is in need of soldiers" He clapped Jeremy on the shoulder and said, "I'm like to enlist my son, Thaddeus."

22

CHARLOTTE

ON THE TRIP BACK TO THE HOUSE, WE ALL AGREE WE need to tell Lily the truth. She is Jeremy's kin after all. It feels cruel not telling her. Besides, now we have proof that we found Jeremy's home.

"My, my, my!" Lily says when I finish telling her my story of meeting Jeremy.

"My, my, my," she repeats when we show her the quilt and the pile of letters between Laurie and John Turner about Jeremy's disappearance and explain that we'd like to show them to Jeremy. Lily sits stunned, staring over the field.

"Lily," Eric says. "Is there something you want to tell us?"

Lily looks Eric in the eyes and seems to be mulling something over. She chews on her lower lip for a minute.

"You three have been honest with me," she says finally. "I appreciate that. You could have taken these things and I'd be none the wiser. What I'm about to say, I haven't told anyone, my whole life. It's been at least 70 years since I've been up in that atic, so I can't say for sure…" She hesitates.

"She's still there, isn't she, Lily?" Eric's voice is hushed and gentle. Lily looks at Eric and then at me. She nods.

"When I was a child, my grandmother told me that her mother's ghost waited by the old farmhouse gate. I didn't believe her. You know old people. They're always saying crazy things. But one evening I was riding my favorite pony, Patches, past the old shed. It was just before dusk. There used to be a little bit of the old fence post there still then. We were walking kind a slowly, not making much noise when I saw a woman in the field, wearing an long loose dress that was sort of billowing around her knees. But the day was so hot, and there wasn't any breeze.

"As I approached her, she turned and looked at me. Her eyes looked so sad it just about broke my heart. Then before I could do a thing, she vanished, right in front of me. I never saw her again, and I never mentioned it to anyone. Deep down in my heart, I knew it was my great-grandmother looking for Jeremy. It's the reason I never sold that field or moved out of this run-down house. I felt obliged to let her keep her vigil, undisturbed."

I look at Eric. "Do you think...?" I don't finish my sentence.

Josh jumps in. "It's got to be her. She's been waiting all this time."

"According to my grandmother, during her whole life, her mother never gave up watching for that boy. She wasn't the kind of woman to let a little thing like dying get in her way."

I swallow the lump in my throat. In the five months since Dad died, I haven't stopped thinking it will be him on the phone when it rings. It still stings every time a white Ford pickup drives by. I *know* Dad isn't coming back. I can't imagine what it must have been like for Jeremy's mother.

"What now?" I ask.

"We show him that quilt," Eric says. "Then we step back and see what happens."

"We have to try," I say. "Would you like to read the letters?" I hold out the stack we found.

Lily shakes her head. "You take them, child, my eyes are too blurry just now to read them."

"My, my, my. You children sure have taught an old lady a thing or two."

She pauses, then touches her heart with her hand. "And to think ... Just about breaks your heart to think of that boy lost and alone all this time...." her voice trails off. Lily's eyes glisten with tears and she presses her lips together. She nods but doesn't speak.

The three of us hardly utter a word until we're sitting on our bikes at the corner near school.

"You guys, I cannot do this by myself," I say finally.

"Dude! No way I'm missing this," Eric says, smiling from ear to ear.

Jeremy

August 29, 1862 Manassas, Virginia

Jeremy lay back against the hillock. He'd rest a minute. He needed to reload. A searing pain in his side made him wince.

A second ago, he'd stood up to fire when he saw a flash and something rammed into him with the force of a bull. He never even saw the soldier standing there. Damn Rebel had hit him before he had a chance to fire. He probed his side. He couldn't sit up. Sticky warmth flowed over his hand. He lifted it and his fingers were covered in bright red blood.

Next to him, another soldier knelt, aiming his gun over the top of the berm. Smoke drifted just over his head. A splash of dirt rained down on them from the top of the hill.

He and his company had marched for days. Each night when the captain had signaled the end of the day's march, Jeremy dropped his pack, disentangled himself from his canteen and rifle, and slumped to the ground.

Some nights, he hadn't moved and fell asleep right where he had fallen.

"I'm hit," Jeremy said to the soldier beside him. The other man didn't answer. He leapt up over the edge of the hill and was gone. The sound of guns and cannon rattled inside Jeremy's head. He leaned against the dirt and closed his eyes. He'd rest, just for a minute.

He woke to the feeling of being lifted by the shoulders and feet. Someone was moving him. Light fluttered and he felt a searing heat in his side.

"Water." He licked his cracked lips. They tasted of gunpowder and sweat. The world swirled as pain surged through him. Whoever had lifted him, released him as his back and head touched the ground.

There was a tugging at his shirt. Someone talking.

"Stop!" Was that croak his voice?

"How bad is he?" Muffled voices conferred above his head. They sounded far away.

"Get him to the rear." Hands pushed under his shoulders. Around his ankles.

They lifted him again. Pain tensed his body as the weight of his legs pulled at the tear in his side, knowing only pain. Then blackness.

When he came to again, the noise around him sounded like it was inside his head. He shivered. It was so cold. Something moved in the firelight behind him.

"Water." His voice grated at the back of his throat.

A face appeared above him. A girl. "Water, please." She smiled at him and lifted his head. Water trickled in his throat and down his neck. Cool water against a burning thirst. A hand pressed a wet cloth against his forehead.

"There you are, soldier. Rest now."

"Tell Ma."

"You can tell her yourself when you see her." The voice was bright and young. "You're going home, soldier."

I gotta tell her.

"Did you get his name and kin?" A voice came from behind him. He couldn't see the face.

Hands ruffled through his pockets and across his chest. The rustle of papers. "Thaddeus Crouch. From Pennsylvania."

Thaddeus. The name sounded familiar. A thread of memory hung just out of reach. "Collect his effects, record what he says. Try to make him comfortable."

He struggled to see, who they were they talking about. "Rest now, Thaddeus. Drink some water."

No. Not Thaddeus.

"I'm…Jeremy," he said with a gasp.

"What's that he's mumbling?"

He struggled to look at who was speaking. He tried to twist. Where was she? His heart raced as the world swirled around him.

"I'm not Thaddeus." His body wouldn't move. The effort sent a new wave of pain through him.

He drew a breath. "I'm..." His voice was just a whisper. "I'm..." It sounded far away. He felt himself slipping. Blackness rose around his shoulders and covered his face.

He had to tell them.

His breath rattled in his chest, pain seized him, and then all went silent.

23

CHARLOTTE

I STAND AT THE WATER FOUNTAIN OF THE MANASSAS Battlefield visitor's center, gripping Beau's leash in one hand. In the other is a plastic grocery bag with the ancient, folded baby quilt. Josh and Eric sit on the hood of the Eric's sister's old Mustang in the parking lot twenty feet away. Eric wrangled his sister to help. She watches from the driver's seat. My heart gallops as if I'd been sprinting.

The sun, hanging low over the far end of the battlefield, makes the sky look like it's blushing. It will be dark in about an hour. The park is on the verge of closing.

I take a deep breath and walk around the side of the building. And there Jeremy sits.

Waiting.

Beau lunges just as Jeremy turns to face me. He hugs my dog as Beau licks his face. I let go of Beau's leash, and slowly walk up behind him. I stroke Beau's back.

"Jeremy," I say.

He doesn't move. He nuzzles his face into the dog's neck and squeezes harder.

"I want to show you something."

Calmly, I take the quilt out of the plastic grocery bag. It falls open with the smell of ancient fabric. Confusion, then recognition fill Jeremy's eyes. He reaches his hand toward the quilt.

"She didn't want me to fight."

"I'll take you home."

At that moment, a park ranger rounds the building. I gasp and Jeremy vanishes.

"I'm sorry, miss. You'll have to get moving now. The park is closing."

I can't believe it! He ruined everything.

"Let's go, Beau," is my only reply.

I storm across the grass to the car. I don't even look at Josh and Eric as I pull on the car door. Eric yanks the front seat forward. Beau hops in. Josh and I follow him.

"Uggghh!" I growl.

Before I can utter the swear word that's forming on the tip of my tongue, a voice whispers, "I left without saying goodbye."

In the front, seat Eric turns to his sister and mouths the word "drive." She looks at me in the rearview mirror, puts the car in gear, and eases out of the parking space.

My knuckles are white from gripping Beau's leash and the bag holding the quilt. I pray this works.

24

CHARLOTTE

By the time we pull up in front of Lily's house, my breath is shallow and fast. No one said a word the entire drive. Thank God for HOV lanes at rush hour. Eric's sister goes 70, and we make it in 15 minutes. Now, as we pull up to the curb, I take a deep breath.

Here we go.

We went over it all in the car at the Battlefield. "He won't recognize the house," Eric said. "You'll have to lead him around back. Whatever you do, don't let go of Beau or the quilt."

Josh nods at me as he holds the seat forward. "This is gonna work, you'll see," he says.

I close my eyes, take a deep breath, nod at Eric and Josh, then slowly climb out of the car. Beau scrambles out of the back seat, his tail high and wagging frantically.

I follow my dog's stare and see Jeremy standing on the front lawn. He looks at Lily's decrepit house. She appears at the front door. Standing at her side, scratching to get out is Colonel. Beau's tail wags faster.

"Eric?" Josh says.

"I see him," Eric whispers. "Let him be. He doesn't know where he is yet."

"You see him?" I ask.

Josh nods once in response.

Lily steps out the front door and Colonel dashes out past her, barking and leaping at the boy like he's happy to see him. Jeremy seems to take no notice of the large dog. Beau pushes past me and squeezes through the half-open gate, taking his leash with him.

Lily stares at the young man on her lawn. Her eyes fill with recognition. She covers her mouth with shaking hands and glances from Jeremy to me. I nod slowly at her.

Jeremy moves toward the side of the house.

"Colonel, you old coot, hush!" Lily scolds the dog. Her voice sounded fragile.

Halfway around the house, Jeremy stops. He stares at the gnarled tree in the center of the side yard, just inside the fence.

"Yes, it's the old elm," Lily says. Jeremy turns his head slowly to look at her. "You're home, Jeremy." Her voice cracks as tears stream down her cheeks.

Beau rushes straight toward Colonel and the two dogs sniff each other. Without warning, Colonel bolts toward the back garden. Jeremy disappears.

Lily gasps then rushes off the porch following the dogs. Beau and Colonel race each other to the crest of the hill behind the house. Eric stops first and stares toward the old cabin and the sweeping field beyond it. We stop behind him. Below us in the field the dogs run toward the cabin. But now there are three dogs. Another Black Lab prances in the field with Colonel and Beau. Jeremy stands staring at the cabin.

"Look," Josh whispers. A woman in an ankle length dress, wrapped in a shawl, stares back at Jeremy.

"It's her," Lily says.

"Ma? I'm sorry." Jeremy's voice cracks as if he is fighting tears.

"Jeremy? Is it truly thee?" Even from where we stand, we see tears streaming down her cheeks. Jeremy moves through the tall grass as the woman throws open her arms. Jeremy buries his face in her shoulder. The second Black Lab charges toward them. As the dog approaches, Jeremy pulls gently away from his mother. He turns toward the dog. In that instant, the woman looks up at us. She stares directly into my eyes, touches her heart, and then they are gone.

Lily gasps again. Tears rolls down my cheek and drips off my chin, as I let out the sob I have been holding in. Josh wraps his arm around my shoulder, and we hug. He sniffs. He's crying, too.

Eric, standing alone a few feet in front of the rest of us, wipes the back of his hand across his nose and continues to stare out over the field. He digs his hands into his pockets and hangs his head.

Beau barks three quick barks and then hurries back to-ward Colonel, who lays panting on the ground, his tail beating a frenzied rhythm on the grass.

25

CHARLOTTE

"6:00." THE NUMBERS ON THE CLOCK SEEM TO TAUNT me. It is Saturday, but I have to be at school in thirty minutes. Stonewall Jackson Middle School is hosting the Northern Virginia Invitational. Couldn't we have picked a better time since it's our course?

Today is my first meet since Josh and I were suspended from running. A pang of remorse stirs the old flock of butterflies in my stomach. Coach had barely spoken to me in class the last two weeks, and I couldn't look at him. I let him down.

Today, I'd make it up to him.

I leave a note for mom. "Gone to the meet. Back @ 2."

The night before, as I walked past her door to go to bed, Mom had called me into her room.

"Can I give you a ride tomorrow?" she asked.

"Nah, that's alright. The run over there will be a good warm up."

"Sweetie?" she sounded worried. "Coach Elsberry said you won a medal in your last meet. I saw him when I met with the principal after your suspension. How come you didn't tell me?"

I shrugged. "I guess I thought it was no big deal. It's just a bronze." She cocked her head but didn't say anything else.

Now as I round the corner toward the school driveway, I stop short. Could I have it wrong?

The school is draped in banners, and a balloon arch rises above the far end of the track. "Go Stonewall Jackson," and "Go Raiders" shout banners that seem to cover every inch of fence around the track. It looks like the place is set up for a football game. Just like the day in the picture on our sideboard, the day I had gone back with Dad to his high school for Homecoming.

He had brought me to the game. The band had marched on the field playing the school fight song. I couldn't see, so he hoisted me onto his shoulders. I must have been six or seven, young enough to love being on his shoulders, but old enough to know that he shouldn't have to carry me that way. Someone took our picture and Mom framed it.

In my memory, Dad is young, and it was like being with a celebrity. Everybody knew him and everybody wanted to talk to him. They clapped him on the arm or punched his fist. On his shoulders I felt happy. Safe. I forgot all about the game.

"I saw your dad run fifty yards for a touchdown, dragging defenders on both arms as he crossed the goal line," one guy said to me.

Someone else said, "I ain't seen nobody run like that before or since."

"He sure was fast," they told me. "You should have seen him run."

Sitting on his shoulders I could feel the thrum of his voice and laugh against my legs, the deep bass of it and the strength of his hands holding my ankles. He hummed with pride. At that moment, to me at least, he was holding up the sky.

Then other questions began. "When's the next deployment, Steve? What's it like over there?"

"C.C.. Over here," Josh calls from somewhere behind me. I like that nick-name. It makes me feel at home somehow.

The infield is lined with tables and flags, and people are everywhere. No way this is just for the Cross-Country Team.

The coach and the team are clumped together stretching. Coach sees me and winks. I can't help myself. I smile. Coach Ellsbury seems to have forgotten how mad he was at me.

My heat is one of the last. I didn't expect Coach to put me in the fastest race, since he hadn't seen me run in two weeks.

At the sound of the starting gun, I explode off the line.

The first mile is an easy lope. Other runners surge past me. I've run this route a thousand times. I let my lungs and legs do what they know how to do. They know the roll of the landscape. Let the others kill themselves on the first hill. I check my watch. I'm running just over a six-and a half-minute pace. I step up my effort.

When I run by the Visitor's Center, my heart aches.

No Jeremy.

I round the bend at the bottom of the hill. A few of the runners in front of me slow as they head up Henry House Hill.

I surge forward. As I crest the hill at the cannons, my heart feels like some crazy band is playing it's heart out in my chest. My lungs scream for air.

The wall behind the Visitors' Center is empty.

He's home.

I head down the Battlefield drive. The homestretch. Words echo in my mind before I can stop them.

"It's Dad," Mom had said that day in the school hallway.

I gasp at a sudden sting of grief and stumble. Who will help Dad to make it home?

The wind whistles past my ears, as memories of us playing checkers and softball, eating breakfast, and running flood my mind.

My heart seems to rise out of my chest as I remember his voice saying "I love you, C.C." a million times over Skype and kissing me before turning off the light at night when he was home.

Tears sprout at the corners of my eyes, but I don't slow down.

I turn up Sudley Road. A bright blue sky seems to pull me forward and now it's as if my entire body is airborne, as if the memory of Dad's voice is making me fly. I move through the pack of runners, see only their shoes, feel only my breath, and my heart pounding. Then they're behind me.

Flags and banners flutter in the wind as I run toward the open gate of the football field for the final lap around the track. Faces come into focus, kids from the cafeteria and my classes.

Their eyes are all on me, and I sprint like I've never sprinted before. The faint echo of a loudspeaker squeaks out my name.

"And number 104, our own Charlotte C.C. Cross is in the lead for the girls!" People are cheering my name. "Cee Cee, Cee Cee." When did everybody start calling me C.C.? I hear Josh's voice leading the cheer.

The crowd lines the track. My heart and legs throb. My arms pump. The sensation of leaving my body, rising above the crowd lifts me. At that moment something else tugs at me. The crowd noises fade and I hear something that's only a whisper.

"Run, C.C., run." It's Dad's voice filling my heart and my head as if he's running beside me. I sprint toward the finish line, as a wall inside me bursts. Anger, sorrow, relief, and joy all carry me forward like I'm riding on the crest of a giant, hurtling wave.

The voice on the loudspeaker calls me back. "Charlotte is a 7th grader at Stonewall Jackson Middle School. She's the daughter of 1991 Stonewall High School graduate and four-letter wide receiver for the Raiders, Steven Cross. She's showing some of that famous Cross speed here today, folks; let's cheer her in." They're talking about Dad. About me.

I have no idea who else is around me. My whole body yearns for the yellow tape ahead. It stretches across the track, beckoning to me like a promise. A few more steps. I lunge forward.

The tape presses against me, then releases, and I burst through. I thrust my hands into the air and run with my head back, my heart pounding like an animal that wants out of its cage.

As I slow, the crowd comes back into focus. People all around me scream. Feet stomp on the metal stands. Faces bounce beside the fence that lines the infield. Someone calls to me near the front of the crowd. Mom pushes forward with her arms over her head, celebrating. She's here. She saw.

I run to her. She bends forward over the fence, reaches her arms around me. The fence presses into my legs and waist. In that moment, as I melt into my mother, I feel Dad's arms around us, too, just like we hugged when he came home. Tears gather in my eyes, and I give in to let the sob pour out.

"I miss him, Mom."

"I know, Sweetie." She rubs my back. "I miss him, too." My chest heaves with a deep breath in. "He would be…is proud of you."

I can't move. I don't want to break the sensation of his strong arms around my mother and me. It feels so real.

"C.C., you did it. You set a record!" It's Josh. "Amazing race, C.C." Coach's voice now, too.

I step back, quickly wipe my eyes. I laugh. It sounds like it used to sound, familiar. Like it sounded the day Dad lifted me to his shoulders at Homecoming when I was six.

Then my team swarms me. They pound me on the back, scream in my face, throw their arms around me.

"You broke the track record, C.C. By five seconds.

"You did it!"

"That was amazing!"

My heart feels like it will jump out of my chest. I close my eyes, lean my head back and speak to him again in my head.

Dad. Wherever you are, I know you know. I know you saw. I love you, Dad.

Then, as people press in around me on all sides, silent words form in my mind, like a swirling voice without sound.

"I love you too, C.C. I love you too."

Acknowledgment

A special thank you, from the bottom of my heart, to Alec Simone, Kathleen Simone, Amei Myer, and Sharyn Miller for all you have done to bring this book to life.

Discussion Questions

How did the author's choice to tell the story from both C.C.'s and Jeremy's perspectives influence the story?

Did it make it easier or harder to understand events in history and their lives? Why?

What parallels between C.C.'s and Jeremy's lives might have helped them connect with one another?

How are their lives different? How do their differences influence their decisions.

How do lies change the lives of both C.C. and Jeremy?

With which characters in the novel do you most identify? How?

At school, C.C. has trouble making friends, why?

What might you feel starting a new school?

How might you have helped her?

Jeremy's life on a farm in the 1860s is very different from modern farms.

How?

How is Jeremy's life harder than yours?

How is it easier?

How is Jeremy's society affected by war?

What was the United States Civil War fought over?

Does the U. S. Civil War have an impact on the United States today? How?

Who are the Quakers, or the Society of Friends as they call themselves?

The Friends' Peace Testimony says:

"***We utterly deny all outward wars and strife and fightings with outward weapons, for any end, or under any [pretense] whatsoever; and this is our testimony to the whole world. The spirit of Christ, by which we are guided, is not changeable, ... and so [we] testify to the world, that the spirit of Christ, which leads us into all Truth, will never move us to fight and war against any man with outward weapons, neither for the kingdom of Christ, nor for the kingdoms of this world.***"

What does this statement mean to Jeremy and his family?
To you?
To your family?

What is the author's view on war? How does that view effect the story?

More stories set during the U. S. Civil War.

Soldier's Heart: Being the Story of the Enlistment and Due Service of the Boy Charley Goddard in the First Minnesota Volunteers, by Gary Paulson

Across Five Aprils, Irene Hunt

Stealing Freedom, by Elisa Carbone

Moon Over Tennessee: A Boy's Civil War Journal, by Craig Crist-Evans, Bonnie Christensen (Illustrations)

Dear America: When Will This Cruel War Be Over?: The Civil War Diary of Emma Simpson, Gordonsville, Virginia, 1864, by Barry Denenberg

The Girls of Gettysburg, by Bobbi Miller

Captured! A Boy Trapped in the Civil War, by Mary Blair Immel

Riot, by Walter Dean Myers

Silent Thunder, by Andrea Davis Pinkney

Bull Run, by Paul Fleischman

www.ingramcontent.com/pod-product-compliance
Lightning Source LLC
LaVergne TN
LVHW090518110826
845146LV00003B/899